Totally Bound Publishing books by Jorja Lovett

The Department Store
Ground Floor: Toys and Games

THE WILD IRISH WOLVES
Volume One

The Wolf on the Hill

The Wolf on the Run

JORJA LOVETT

The Wild Irish Wolves Volume One
ISBN # 978-1-78184-680-3
©Copyright Jorja Lovett 2013
Cover Art by Posh Gosh ©Copyright 2013
Interior text design by Claire Siemaszkiewicz
Totally Bound Publishing

THE WOLF ON THE HILL

Dedication

'Wolfie', as I lovingly refer to this book, came about after a research trip with my long-suffering husband. The Northern Irish countryside is truly inspiring, and only improved by having wonderful company to enjoy it with.

As always, my gratitude goes to my crit group, UCW, who have supported, and bullied, me until I finished this manuscript. I must also name check Cherie in particular for all her hard work on my web and blog, and for dragging me into the twenty-first century.

Thanks also to my lovely editor and the staff at Totally Bound who have made this such a fun experience.

Chapter One

Rain soaked Mia's fur as she bounded through the woods bordering the Olcan Hills, relishing every inch of earth mashed beneath her claws. Trees became nothing more than a blur as she raced by, running to find her release out here where she answered to no one but nature. This was freedom.

When she reached the top of the hill she came to a standstill and released her primal scream of frustration in a howl, unleashing everything she couldn't say to her overbearing family, pouring every hidden truth of who she really was into one long mournful call.

In the distance, another wolf echoed her cry and answered with one of his own. This was the reason her mother despised her shifting into her wolf form. She went kind of crazy and forgot all sense of danger in the excitement. Exactly the reason why she did it in secret. And now, here she was, totally exposed in the Northern Irish countryside, crouched and listening out for the intruder's approach.

Snapping twigs and rustling leaves marked his stealthy journey towards her but she stood her ground, regardless of how loudly her heart was beating in her ears. The wind carried his scent and raised the hackles along her spine when she sniffed the air. Another shifter, but one she didn't recognise. Big bro would use her pelt for a rug if he found out she'd strayed beyond the boundary.

Amber eyes glowed in the dark shadows as the large grey wolf stalked through the forest. She bowed in submission. Even if she had a clue how to fight, he was double her size and twice as powerful. He growled a low warning and sniffed her with interest, his wet nose nudging her clammy fur. Did he expect her to roll over and show her belly? Pride wouldn't let her, but she was careful not to make eye contact as he circled around her twice in case he took it as a challenge.

She only lifted her head when she saw him pad away, heading back to the cover of the trees. He stopped, looked back at her, and cocked his head to one side. When she didn't move he returned and nipped her ear. She yelped in surprise and indignation. Of all the nerve!

The rules of engagement were abandoned in the heat of her outrage and, in a snarling frenzy, she launched herself at him. For an animal so large, the grey wolf moved gracefully, dodging her attack to race ahead and leaving Mia in dogged pursuit.

Tree branches tore at her skin as she ploughed heedlessly into the woodland, but the pain dulled in the exhilaration of the chase. As they wove their way through the undergrowth, Mia's anger subsided to let her long-neglected sense of fun take over.

He wanted her to follow him. She knew that from the glances he kept throwing back at her. So she stopped and slipped quietly behind the stump of an uprooted oak, waiting to see what he would do. White wisps of steam escaped from her nostrils as she fought to get her breath back and suddenly the area seemed too quiet.

With a thud Grey leapt onto the tree stump, and leant back onto his haunches ready to pounce. Mia took off again and this time she was the hunted. She didn't get very far before he sprang and knocked her off her feet.

In a tangle of limbs they rolled through the leafy debris of the forest floor, shifting into their human form as they came to rest, with her pinned to the ground by a hard, muscular, naked body.

"Well, that was fun." He grinned down at her, making no attempt to get off her, his green eyes full of mischief.

"If you say so." Mia's heart still raced but she was at enough of a disadvantage wedged underneath him without admitting she enjoyed the capture as much as the chase.

"I didn't hurt you, did I?" He bent his head to kiss the scratches marking her shoulder and suddenly the only ache she felt was hidden deep inside.

"No." She swallowed hard as he ventured closer to her already puckered nipples.

"Do you want me to stop?" His hot breath on her sensitive skin engulfed her in a tide of hormones she hadn't been ruled by in a long time, if ever.

Maybe a piece of her wolf was still in her system, thriving on the excitement and danger, but she was horny, and ripe for the picking. "No."

With a need to touch, to taste this handsome stranger on her tongue, she manoeuvred enough room to free her hands and wind them into his dark blond hair, pulling him down into a kiss.

He massaged her breasts, first with his hand, quickly followed by his mouth. The sucking and licking around her straining pink tips made her arousal too great to bear. She writhed against him, wet and waiting, but he let her suffer further still whilst he covered her mounds in tiny, exquisite bites.

Bewitched by the woods and her fantasy lover, she swapped the dull reality of her life for this moment, cavorting like the sort of woodland nymph she longed to be. Someone who lived without fear of consequences or judgement.

She wanted him. Prim and proper Mia Blake, who never stepped out of line, was lying naked in the woods with a stranger's erection pressing into her abdomen, and she loved it. A restlessness seized hold as her body cried out with need. Her limbs trembled, her fingers and toes curled, waiting for that final act of completion. As dusk settled around them and an ethereal fog swirled between the trees, she lost herself in the erotic dream and let him sink into her.

With a moan she parted her thighs. He thrust into her, the sheer size of him making her gasp as her body adjusted to fit around him, but she quickly accepted him, welcoming him again and again. The missing part of her femininity slotted into place with every fill of his cock inside her. So this was what all the fuss was about? Up until now sex hadn't been something she had often thought about or had particularly enjoyed. Merely a necessity she'd endured to keep her ex happy. Not like this all-consuming lust heating her from the inside out. Now she knew how it could be, how sensual she could feel, she wouldn't settle for anything less.

"You're so wet." Obviously her partner was enjoying the benefits of her sexual awakening. He levered himself up, locking his arms out straight to look deep into her eyes. Mia gave a shiver at seeing the undisguised desire darkening his pupils, realising she was having the same effect on him as he was on her.

"It is raining." Unaccustomed to this level of intensity, she gave a nervous laugh that jiggled her body against his.

"Christ, you feel so good." He ignored her feeble attempt at mis-timed humour, and thankfully concentrated on the physical aspect of their pairing. The empowerment of discovering her own sexuality, and having it appreciated by a second party, only increased her new appetite for all things thrusty.

"Mmm." She closed her eyes and surrendered to his lead, listening to the growls as he drove into her. Was there ever a more erotic sound than a man claiming her with such beautiful savagery? She doubted it. In response to his primal grunts, her inner cave woman adopted every position she could to drive him deeper inside her.

When he withdrew, the loss was great, her frustration immeasurable. "What are you doing?" she asked, struggling to sit up, her limbs weak from the exertion.

"Turn over." The order coupled with the devilish glint in his eyes melted away what few inhibitions remained. She was his to command when he could carry her to such amazing heights.

Scrambling onto her knees, she complied, but not without question. "Why?"

"I want to take you from behind." His sultry breath in her ear, he knelt behind her so her buttocks rested on his thighs, his rigid flesh pressing into her back.

"Doggie style?" She swallowed hard, not quite knowing what to expect with her limited experience.

"Wolfie style." Mia could almost hear the grin in his voice and braced herself for whatever he had in mind.

He slid a hand up her back and gently coaxed her over onto all fours. One glorious push brought him back home and renewed her contentment as they joined together. The full feeling of having him inside her, with his fingers digging into her hips as he pumped away, sent Mia soaring onward to that peak of bliss.

He reached around to stroke her clit, his digits nudging deep inside to mirror every fill of his cock. Sparks flashed behind her closed eyelids and her breathing grew ragged until she could hold back no more. She came with a cry that echoed through the forest, followed quickly with Grey's howl of release.

Once they had exorcised every residual tremor, they collapsed into a panting, sweaty heap.

"That was just..."

"Animal?" Mia offered, her head still spinning from the intense orgasm.

He laughed and rolled over so they were face to face. The golden stubble lining his tanned jaw made him ruggedly handsome, a deadly combination with the soulful green eyes staring back at her. That puppy dog look could be enough for a woman to fall for him, even without first-hand knowledge of his sexual prowess.

"I was gonna say amazing but yeah, animal works too."

The rain reminded her that this was no dream. As the droplets of reality splashed on her exposed skin, Mia became all too aware of her nakedness and the wanton open air display. Self-awareness swept in quickly for someone who found even wearing a bikini in public traumatic, so she covered her modesty as best she could with two hands.

She didn't know the protocol for making a gracious exit after a quick bunk-up, especially when she was still starkers. He didn't strike her as the type for flowery words anyway, so she kept it short and to the point. "Thanks, but I...er, have to go."

He lay back and watched as she scrabbled to her feet. "That's it? No cuddles?"

"I'm sure you won't shed any tears over it." They'd both got what they'd wanted so she saw no need to pretend it had been anything more than a physical release. Mia, however, was left with tumultuous emotions not so easily dealt with. Another moment of madness had thrown her carefully ordered world into chaos and made her question who exactly she was, and why she denied herself these flashes of happiness.

Mia shifted back into her wolf, and, with one last lingering look at her playmate lying magnificently naked on a bed of leaves, she ran towards the woods. Back to the life she was supposed to lead.

* * * *

The stale stench of cigarettes and alcohol assaulted Caleb's nostrils on opening the door. The smell of home.

A tentative step took him into the dark hallway and onto the wooden floor, tacky beneath his boots. The air was still, heavy with neglect and abuse, and it took every ounce of courage for him not to turn around and walk straight back out.

Instead, he carried on into the living room and opened the window to invite a blast of cool autumnal wind to sweep through the gloom. Something crunched underfoot and he knelt to inspect the damage. Glass. Beer bottles to be exact, littering the floor along with cigarette packets and food remnants. He turned up his nose, even though he should've expected it. Every stray wolf that happened along always used this place as an unofficial pack house. His father welcomed everyone with open arms. Except his own son, of course.

Ironic now that, as next of kin, Caleb had inherited this very house where his father had made his life a living hell. Viewing the destruction around him, Caleb wondered what chaos had reigned in his eleven-year absence. The yellowing paper on the walls, once decorated with pretty spring flowers, now featured slogans and expletives daubed in bright red paint. The old brown sofa was slashed open, stuffing ripped from its guts and strewn around the floor, and there was an empty space in the corner where the television had once sat.

A niggling thought crawled inside his head and a quick look around the rest of the house confirmed his suspicions. Every room revealed new devastation and vandalism. With doors hanging from their hinges, drawers ransacked and every electrical appliance ripped from the walls, this was more than the aftermath of a pack party.

He booted a discarded beer can across the floor. "Fuck!"

Too many ghosts had held Caleb back from taking occupancy earlier and now his plans were royally screwed. So much for a quick sale.

"Hello? Is there someone in there?" a deep voice bellowed from the hall.

Shit! He had forgotten to lock the door behind him, but he suspected that burglars didn't announce themselves before they robbed you blind. Besides, there was nothing left to take.

Caleb didn't answer but edged his way cautiously along the wall to peer around the corner. A dark figure loomed large but Caleb Jackson didn't back down from a fight, even with an opponent built like the side of a house. His wolf growled a warning, low and deep.

"Caleb? Is that you? It's me, Rory."

It took a moment for the name to register, but he recognised the would-be intruder the minute he stepped into the small shaft of light escaping through the door. Rory Blake, high school hero, all round good guy and the constant reminder of everything Caleb had lacked when they were growing up. A real blast from the past, and his past was the very thing he wanted to avoid.

"What brings you here, Rory?"

"I saw the bike outside and I know the house has laid empty since your father died." He shrugged his broad shoulders.

The fact that he gave a shit irked Caleb all the more. "Pity the neighbourhood watch wasn't more vigilant before now."

Rory peered behind him to survey the debris. "You know how remote these hills are. If I'd known…"

"What business is it of yours anyway?" Caleb's last nerve snapped at having Golden Boy witness the pitiful legacy left to him by his father. He wouldn't be surprised if the whole thing turned out to be a set-up by the old bastard in a last stab at humiliating him. After running away from the abusive home at the age of sixteen, the discovery of the inheritance had been bittersweet. Now, it was just plain bitter.

"I'm a police officer." Rory's words were spoken with pride but also a hint of irritation. A burglary on his doorstep probably didn't sit well with PC Perfect.

"So you're the law round these here parts?" It figured. "I'm sure you're a real credit to the police service of Northern Ireland." Caleb didn't bother to hide the sarcasm in his exaggerated drawl. He and authority did not make for good bedfellows.

Rory's eyes narrowed, his wolf shining through for a brief moment. "I'm also the alpha now."

Another non-surprise, but at least Rory deserved the respect shown to the pack leader, unlike Caleb's father.

He opened his arms wide in an act of submission. "Hey, I've got no problem with that. I'm not about to challenge you. As soon as I get this place on the market, I'm outta here. Though I guess it's gonna take longer than I thought now."

And cost him every penny he had to put it right.

"I can ask around, see if anyone saw who did this and dust for prints." Rory remained professional but Caleb knew it was a waste of time.

"Forget it. They've had months to fence whatever they took and there have been more people through here than the Europa bus station. I'll get it put to rights as soon as I can and move on."

Rory nodded, the plan obviously to his liking as well.

"Rory, I'm freezing sitting out in that car. Can we go yet?" A female voice breached the male stronghold, followed by a familiar face. Only hours earlier he'd chased her stunning white wolf form through the nearby woods. Her face paled as she recognised him and Caleb's inner wolf howled in appreciation at being reunited with its mate.

His human couldn't complain either. Slim, slight and blonde, she was every man's fantasy. Although he preferred her naked instead of the jeans and jumper cover-all she wore now.

"Caleb, you remember my sister Mia?"

Holy shit! He'd just fucked Rory Blake's little sister six ways to Sunday!

"Yes, I think I recognise her." He swept his eyes over her body, remembering how responsive she had been to his touch.

"Caleb?" Large blue eyes blinked at him in fear. As if he would rat her out to her brother and run the risk of having his balls handed to him on a plate for his trouble.

"I told you to wait in the car." Rory let his cool demeanour slide to scold his baby sister but Caleb was too caught up in this latest revelation to crow over it.

"Maybe I'm sick of being told what to do." Mia pursed her pretty pink lips, reminding him of the pigtailed nuisance that used to follow him around like a shadow when they were kids. He never did understand her fascination with him, figuring that the pampered princess got her kicks watching a guy fail at life on a daily basis. Well, now she'd had her bit of rough and he'd got to enjoy the sweet revenge of watching embarrassment stain her cheeks.

Rory glanced at both of them in turn and scowled. "It's late. I have to get Mia home. I'll round up some help tomorrow but in the meantime you can stay at mine."

"No!" Caleb and Mia chorused together.

"Thanks, but I don't think your folks would appreciate a house guest at such short notice." Caleb could imagine the mighty Blakes' reaction to him revving up to the estate and messing up their perfectly manicured driveway.

"I've got my own place now and you can't stay here without heat." Rory wrapped his knuckles on one of the radiators hanging from the wall. "I owe you for not keeping a closer eye on the place."

Caleb mulled the offer over. He was pretty sure his wolf would save him from the cold and he was used to kipping on sofas, or roaming the woods in his animal guise. The thought of being in Saint Rory's debt didn't sit well with him either. Then again, the expression of horror on Mia's face was proving irresistible to his bad boy tendencies.

"Well, if you insist." The sadistic streak running in his veins made him accept. The change in her, from the rampant sexual dynamo who'd had her legs slung over his shoulders so he could fuck her that much harder, to this diffident replica, didn't sit easily with him. If she thought she could treat him like a lesser mortal now just because he'd dared to enter her cosseted kingdom, she could think again.

He gave them his cheesiest grin and decided he may as well have a little fun while being forced to confront his past.

Chapter Two

"I didn't know we served ice cream floats in here." Naomi cocked an eyebrow at Mia across the bar.

She frowned. Of course they didn't serve kiddie drinks in this hard liquor pub. Mia shut off the pump and lifted the pint of beer. Only then did she understand the jibe.

"Oh. Sorry." The foamy head half filled the pint glass. The customers who frequented The Wild Dog would surely have lynched her if she'd tried to serve it to them.

Under her boss's watchful eye Mia corrected her mistake and served a full pint of golden lager to a relieved regular.

Naomi's features softened into a smile. "You seem distracted this morning."

"Just something on my mind." *Or someone.* Mia turned her attention back to retrieving the glasses from the dishwasher, trying not to linger on thoughts of reckless carnal acts or sexy bad boys. It didn't work. Even now she swore she could smell his heady, earthy scent, reminding her of his naked body pressed tightly to hers. The glass she was holding slipped from her fingers and smashed to smithereens on the tiled floor as her daydream claimed her attention.

"Shit!"

Naomi sighed and fetched a dustpan and brush to clean up the mess. "Do you want to share this mind-melting problem before you put me out of business?"

"It's fine." *Damn Caleb Jackson!* She didn't get flustered and she sure as hell didn't let her personal problems affect her in public. She blamed him completely for her total work fail. Until yesterday, the last time she'd set eyes on him he'd been a scruffy teenager on the receiving end of a beating from his father. Now her sympathy for Caleb Jackson was definitely being overshadowed by thoughts of a more risqué nature.

Thankfully, the lunchtime crowd began to filter in and Naomi dropped the inquisition to play hostess.

"Hey, sis." Somewhere among the crowd, Rory had managed to slip in unnoticed. Her brother possessed that annoying knack of showing up when she least wanted to talk.

He stretched across the bar to reach for a menu, though Mia didn't know why he bothered.

"I'll have the soup of the day and a coffee," he ordered, like he didn't have the same thing every day.

He pretended to study the menu but Mia saw the sly glimpses he snatched at Naomi. She grinned. Her macho big brother still hadn't worked up the courage to ask the attractive brunette out after two years of pining for her, but Mia knew better than to interfere. Naomi kept her private life closely guarded. No one knew anything of her background, save for the fact that she had turned up in town, heavily pregnant, and with enough money to buy the pub outright. Anyone who questioned her about her past was quickly dispatched with a flea in their ear, and Mia's problems were great enough without adding her boss's wrath to the mix.

"So, um, did your new lodger settle in okay?" She turned her back to pour a black coffee so Rory couldn't read her as easily as she read him.

"Yeah. I'm thinking of getting a work party together to help him sort his place out. You in?"

She almost suffered third degree coffee burns at the idea of working alongside Caleb. Caught up in the euphoria of her liberation as a wolf, she'd willingly gone into his arms, unaware that her actions would come back to haunt her so close to home. Mr Jackson certainly couldn't provide the security her parents expected from a suitor. She would do well to forget him altogether.

"In what?" Naomi walked in on the end of their conversation to place a bowl of steaming hot tomato and basil soup in front of Rory. "Are you two planning a bank job or something?" The smiles exchanged between her brother and her boss left Mia out in the cold, yearning for a share of the warmth emanating between them.

"The old Jackson place on the hill was vandalised. I'm looking for volunteers to help fix it up." Rory's face, so full of hope, concentrated on Naomi's response.

"I will if Mia will." Naomi threw her under the bus. There was no way Mia could say no now and refuse the big eejit some quality time with the love of his life.

"Sure. There's nothing better I'd like to do in my spare time than freeze my arse off in a derelict house with a mop in my hand." *Or spend the whole time pretending I didn't bonk the house owner like a wild thing.*

The sarcasm was lost on her too-far-gone-to-notice sibling.

"Great. Hey, Caleb. We've got our first two recruits."

Another glass hit the deck when Caleb appeared from the gents' bathroom.

"Mia, what the hell is wrong with you today?" Naomi pushed her shell-shocked employee to one side and proceeded to sweep up for the second time.

"Are you sickening for something?" Rory studied her with concern, probably getting ready to bundle her up in cotton wool and ship her straight home to mother.

Mia didn't have the chance to make up an excuse as Caleb walked straight into her eye line with a smirk that described his every dirty thought in great detail, sending her hormones haywire and making her panties wet.

"Yeah, you do look kinda hot."

"I think something must have disagreed with me," she mumbled, wishing Caleb could be a gentleman for once and let the matter drop.

"You sure about that?" He sniffed the air and she saw a flash of amber fire in his eyes. *Oh holy hell! Surely he can't smell my arousal?*

"You know what? I probably should go home. Sorry, Naomi. I'll be back as soon as I get this out of my system." Glaring daggers at Olcan Hills' latest resident, Mia took off her apron and admitted defeat.

"Sure. Maybe you could bring some plastic cups for your next shift?" Naomi snarked, emptying another panful of glass shards into the dustbin.

"Do you want me to give you a lift home?" Rory pushed his food aside and attempted to get up from his seat.

"No thanks. I'll walk. The fresh air might do me some good." With the usually homely log fire burning nearby now seeming unbearably hot and the cosy bar suddenly claustrophobic, she just wanted out of there. Away from Caleb Jackson's smouldering looks and I'm-picturing-you-naked smile.

As had become his recent habit, Caleb jumped in to upset her plans. He put a hand on Rory's shoulder to restrain him in the chair. "Don't worry, I'll see Mia home. You stay and finish your lunch."

"But... But..." *Think, damn it!* She fought for an excuse to decline the son of a bitch's magnanimous offer, while Caleb calmly took her by the elbow and steered her towards the door.

"I insist. Your brother knows you're in safe hands with me."

Left with no choice but to go with him in case she aroused her brother's suspicions, she followed Caleb out, vowing to ditch him as soon as they were out of sight. "If my brother knew what you did to me, he'd have you stuffed and mounted."

"First of all, I didn't hear you complaining about what I did to you. In fact, I think I remember it went more along the lines of, 'That feels so good... Don't stop...'"

She raised a hand, willing him to stop assaulting her with those delicious memories.

He wasn't done. "Stuffed and mounted, you say? You like it that way, don't you, Mia?"

She followed her sharp intake of breath with an exasperated groan and strode ahead down the path. Unfortunately, with only fields and scrub as far as the eye could see, there was no chance of avoiding him.

He jogged up alongside her. "You know, I didn't have you down as a beer and nuts kind of girl. I thought you'd end up spending your days lunching with the well-to-do."

Not for the first time did she find herself having to justify her job. "For your information, I went to medical school, but it wasn't for me. Working at The Dog puts money in my pocket. I can't complain."

He didn't pursue the subject, but went on to tackle the other matter she wished to avoid. "So, are we ever gonna talk about what happened in the woods?"

"No."

"We're gonna pretend it never happened?"

"Exactly." She kept up her brisk pace.

"Really? You're not up for a repeat performance then?"

Mia spun around. The guilt, fear, embarrassment, not to mention longing, spiralling through her body, were emotions she did not wish to court on a regular basis. "It was a mistake. I don't do that... I usually don't do that sort of thing."

"No?" A raised eyebrow questioned her virtue.

"No." She repeated firmly. Someone as obviously promiscuous as Caleb wouldn't understand the significance of that one act to someone like her. The daughter of Edward and Gayle Blake would never dream of behaving in such a manner and running the risk of tarnishing the family's good name. The free-spirited wolf on the other hand apparently got carried away in the heat of the moment.

Fixing her eyes intently on his, she made it plain she had no desire for those two different aspects of her life to intersect and tear her apart. "I don't need the likes of you screwing things up for me."

His face contracted into a frown. "Fine. Just pretend it was nothing more than a bad dream."

She should have felt nothing but relief when he walked away, ending a conversation she hadn't wanted to have in the first place. But a pang of regret lingered with Mia, along with the image of that freshly crushed look on Caleb's face. It wasn't his fault that she wanted to deny her body's natural reaction to him, merely unfortunate that he had ended up on the receiving end of her own self-loathing.

Maybe she could find some way to make it up to him for her brusque behaviour. Preferably something that didn't involve her being in close physical contact with her walking, talking aphrodisiac.

* * * *

Caleb filled bag after bag full of litter from the wreckage of the cottage. After a fitful night's sleep under Rory's roof, replaying Mia's look of contempt in his head, he had risen with the sun and set to work, eager to get the hell out of this place before it dragged him down again.

While he never did go in for hearts, flowers and promises ever after, to have her dismiss him so callously had struck soundly at his ego. It reminded him of his childhood here, unwanted, unloved and an embarrassment to those around him. After years of building up his defences, relying on no one but himself, he didn't intend to hang around waiting for a pampered princess to validate his existence.

The minute the doors of the nearest estate agent had opened that morning, he had put the wheels in motion with a phone call. The fun most definitely over, now he was simply tasked with making the house presentable for viewing.

"Anybody home?" He heard a brief knock quickly followed by the thunder of work boots crossing the threshold. *I really must remember to start locking that door.*

"Hey, Caleb. I've brought a few helping hands for you." Rory, looking mighty pleased with himself, led a procession of workers into his living room.

"Hi, everyone. Thanks for coming." Caleb acknowledged their gracious spirit in helping someone who'd probably pissed them all off at some point in his rebellious teens. He'd done his fair share of petty theft and vandalism, in an attempt to get at his father.

Although, going by the uncomfortable shuffling of feet and furtive glances around him, he imagined they were here for Rory's benefit and not his. He could almost picture a hastily arranged community meeting discussing in hushed tones the best way to oust the bad news biker from the good officer's home. But at least they were all working towards the same goal.

The hairy workmen only appeared vaguely interested in the surroundings when Mia and Naomi appeared alongside them. He wondered what had made his blonde bombshell attend the gathering when she'd seemed so determined to keep him at arm's length. But she'd come dressed for the occasion, wearing black leggings and a baggy blue T-shirt tied in a knot at her waist. With her golden mane swept up into a youthful ponytail, she looked fresh and innocent. Damn it if his libido didn't respond, totally ignoring the fact that she'd seriously dented his pride only yesterday.

She possessed that aura of naïvety that made men want to protect her, as illustrated by the restless natives when Caleb's gaze lingered on her a fraction too long. Brandishing their assorted power tools and brooms, the odd-looking army banded together to protect their queen. The warning came too late. He'd already had his nuts handed to him by the woman herself for thinking he was in with a chance.

"Right." Caleb clapped his hands together, breaking the sudden tension in the room. "Let's get this party started."

The assembled drones worked tirelessly through the day, cleaning and fixing whatever it took to end their responsibility to one of their own. Fair play to Rory, he knew enough tradesmen to make this shell liveable.

"What did you do, threaten them with jail if they didn't help?" Caleb joked with Rory as they worked together to re-hang doors and dump the irreparable furniture.

Rory winced as they hoisted the damaged sofa into the skip, on top of the broken remnants of a table and a dubiously stained mattress. "I'm sure we could rustle up some second-hand furniture for you from somewhere."

"You've done more than enough, mate. Thanks, but I think I can handle things from here." Caleb shrugged off the hand of friendship, not at all comfortable in this unfamiliar territory. In his drifter life, coasting through towns and never lingering long enough to cultivate actual friends, he didn't know how to handle the apparently altruistic policeman. Pats on the back from Rory might have been a sought-after prize for many but they only succeeded in making Caleb suspicious about his motives.

"A word of advice, Caleb. If you want the town to forgive and forget, you've got to learn to do the same." Rory left him to mull that over and carried on with the house clearance.

What the fuck any of it had to do with accepting a second-hand sofa, Caleb didn't know. Letting these people into his house in the first place was the olive branch as far as he was concerned. An entire community who thought he was scum, a woman to whom he was nothing more than an embarrassing indiscretion, and a do-gooder who treated him like a charity case — they were only here to salve their own consciences for turning a blind eye all this time.

He couldn't temper his cynicism, but, when most of the helpers had finished their assigned tasks, even he was forced to admit that the results of the home makeover were impressive. As he walked back through the property, the empty rooms, swept clean of the past and bad memories, were oddly comforting. The coat of magnolia paint the girls had given the place meant that it no longer resembled the vessel for his father's violent rages. The atmosphere now spoke of possibilities, and it seemed to him that the house was calling out to him for a fresh start.

But it would take more than a spring clean to convince him this was the place where he wanted to begin his life over again. Add some respect, a sizeable cash donation, and the love of a good woman, and he'd think about it.

With the living room finished, and Naomi back at the pub for her shift, Mia moved on to decorate one of the bedrooms alone. Singing tunelessly along to the radio, she actually found herself enjoying the task. Maybe she was high on paint fumes, but it gave her a ridiculous sense of achievement to watch the skirting boards transform with a coat of brilliant white gloss under her brush. For now, making sure she covered every inch of wood took her mind off her troubles.

"Oh, it's you singing. I thought there was a cat getting strangled in here." Caleb's sarcasm permeated her solace and she stuck her tongue out at him in childish retaliation.

"You know, this isn't a bad wee place now it's tidied up." Sitting back on her knees to admire her handiwork, she spotted a bare patch in the wood and leant forward to fill it in with a quick swipe of her paintbrush.

"It has a nice view, I'll give you that." He waggled a suggestive eyebrow with his gaze firmly rested on her backside. Another gesture that her body didn't have the courtesy to ignore, as once again her insides turned to mush.

Mia balled up the cloth she had used to mop up any paint spills during her seemingly unnecessary attempt at reconciliation, and tossed it at him. Obviously he wasn't as wounded by the previous day's comments as she'd imagined. "Seriously, though, you could have a nice home here if you wanted."

While the idea of Caleb as a permanent neighbour freaked her out to a certain extent, she believed that, once they put the whole shagging in the forest debacle aside, they could be friends. Ignoring the flirtatious edge to their banter, talking to him made a refreshing change from her now strained conversations with Robbie. If only she hadn't realised too late that he wasn't the one for her. If only her parents would accept her decision.

"I'm not one for settling down." Caleb sounded apologetic, as if he knew the direction her thoughts were headed. "I'll have the house on the market soon. In fact, the estate agent phoned earlier to say there's already an offer."

"Already?" It winded her to find out that he was making plans to hightail it out of there so soon after swooping in and turning her life upside down.

"Yeah. Strange, seeing as it's not even listed yet."

"It's a small community. Word gets around quickly. You should know that." She could have kicked herself for dredging up his past, but thankfully he paid no notice to her slip up.

"That would also go some way to explaining the ridiculously low offer. Obviously someone thought they could get themselves a bargain with the place trashed."

"Surely you're not going to take it?" Mia couldn't explain the sudden panic rising in her chest. If he sold up and moved on, no one would know about her lapse of judgement. *Caleb's quick departure is what I want, isn't it?*

"Not now, no. The house is worth substantially more today than it was yesterday and I can't afford to give it away."

Mia closed the lid on the paint, wiped her brushes and got to her feet. "Well, I'm sure with my artistry you've added at least a tenner to the value."

The pinched expression on his face as he had talked money softened into a smile. As aggravating as he was, she definitely preferred this look on him. "With you in it, the house is priceless."

How quickly a few words, or that particular way he had of looking at her as though she was his entire universe, could revert her back to that carefree spirit he'd first met. For a moment they stood toe to toe with only the buzz of the radio in the background breaking the silence. The airwaves crackled with electricity and Mia held her breath when he reached out to her. Even though her head told her he was all wrong, her body couldn't resist his touch.

He brushed a loose strand of hair from her face and she closed her eyes as anticipation danced along her spine.

His hot breath caressed her skin. "You have something in your hair."

Not exactly the words a girl expected to hear in that moment.

She prised her eyes open and coughed nervously, attempting to expel her mortification. "Paint, I expect. I'm covered in it."

Caleb frowned and examined the locks between his fingers. "No. It's a spider."

"What? Aagh! Get it out! Get it out!" She did the jerky spider dance, trying to expel the offending creature in a series of limb-busting moves.

"It's tiny." Caleb laughed in the face of her hysteria.

"I don't care. It could still crawl into my ear and lay eggs. Get it out!" She sobbed as an involuntary shudder racked through her.

"It's okay." He tugged his fingers through her hair before presenting the specimen for inspection. "See, he's tiny. I'm sure he's more scared of you than you are of him."

"I doubt it." Mia's skin prickled with goose bumps and she was only too glad to see him dispose of the eight-legged beastie through the open window.

"I'm surprised an inoffensive wee creature like that would have such an effect on a wolf shifter."

She hated showing any vulnerability and immediately went on the defensive, folding her arms across her chest. "Everyone has their weakness. Spiders are mine. Okay?" Unwanted tears welled in her eyes and she despised herself for the ridiculous overreaction.

Caleb crossed the room to rest his hands on her shoulders. "Okay. I'm sorry for being an arse about it. We'll say no more on the subject." He wiped away a stray tear with the pad of his thumb and dropped a kiss on her head.

That simple contact was enough to start her free-falling back into that pit of desire. She remembered those lips too well — soft, yet demanding. Her mouth parted on a sigh and she invited him to take a taste.

"I thought you didn't want this." Caleb moved his hands to cup her face and rested his forehead on hers. The hitch in his voice betrayed his struggle for restraint, a quality she did not possess at this moment in time.

"What harm is there in a kiss?" Mia's plea came in a whisper against his lips. Regardless of his good looks and obvious skills in the bedroom department, she knew it was the fact that she could be herself around Caleb that made her act so recklessly. *So why am I spending so much time in my head rather than on his lips?*

The minute their mouths met, animal passion took hold once more, where nothing mattered except exploring her freedom. She lashed her tongue to his, savouring his wild male essence on her every taste bud. Under the flats of her hands, his chest was hard, solid muscle she wanted to take a bite right out of and, suddenly, relying on memories of that wild encounter wasn't enough. She wanted a live action replay.

"Caleb, what are your plans for dinner tonight?" They heard Rory call out from another room moments before he opened the door.

She pushed Caleb away as though he'd burned her, leaving him staggering backward when Rory entered the room. "Ah. There you are. Everyone else appears to have gone home."

Mia pretended to clean her brushes for a second time, stalling for some time to regulate her breathing. That was too close for comfort. Or discomfort. She squirmed with her arousal refusing to dissipate. Her brain might have ended the craziness the minute her brother had intervened, but her spiralling libido wasn't so easily distracted.

"I...er... No plans." Caleb sounded as dazed as she felt, her mind and body foggy with desire.

"Why don't you have dinner with us?"

Mia wanted to throttle her brother, no matter how well-meaning his intentions were. This was definitely one area of her life that didn't need his interference, and she simply didn't trust herself not to offer herself up as dessert if Caleb kept looking at her like that. Self-preservation sent her scrabbling for excuses not to spend any more time with him than necessary.

"Caleb is probably looking forward to getting settled in here. I have a sleeping bag he can borrow and he could order a takeaway." Already struggling to decipher her feelings for Caleb, Rory had trapped her like a wolf in the headlights. Making out was one thing, but cosy family dinners were a step too far. Especially with the exciting new addition of wild beast in a tempting jus to liven up the usually bland menu.

Unfortunately Caleb didn't seem to agree. Pointedly ignoring her ramblings, he slapped her brother on the back. "Cheers, mate. I'd love to have dinner with you guys. I've spent so long on the road I've forgotten how good the taste of home can be."

This time Mia knew that he'd only accepted the invitation to rile her. Okay, so she was weak, she'd kissed him in another moment of vulnerability, but he shouldn't blame her for things beyond her control. Didn't he understand that what she wanted and what she could have were two totally different things?

Clearly not. She shivered beneath his dark stare, which was filled with resentment for spurning him after she'd instigated the kiss. Both a threat and a promise that he wasn't done with her yet.

Chapter Three

The imposing white mansion, complete with stately pillars and veranda, would have looked more at home lording it over a southern plantation than perched atop the bleak Irish hills. But it fitted its purpose in telling the world that the Blakes were somebodies.

"Hello, Mrs Blake." Caleb held out his hand to the elegant blonde who took it limply, regarding him as though he was something her expensive designer shoes had stepped in.

"Hello, Caleb. We heard you were back in town." The familiar blue eyes didn't hold the same warmth as her daughter's.

"Are you going to keep us out on the porch all night?" Rory interrupted his mother's cool appreciation to kiss her on the cheek and push past the parental barricade.

Caleb would have given dinner a miss if he'd known it included the Blake seniors, but, in his desire to get back at Mia for rejecting him again, it had never entered his head. Unused to being the one dangled on a string, this typical drive-thru Romeo certainly didn't do the whole meeting the parents deal. Yet here he was, standing in the hallowed halls of Casa Blake, dressed in his best T-shirt and least oil-stained jeans, feeling every inch the kid from the wrong tracks in a John Hughes movie. His great revenge plan to make Mia squirm had backfired spectacularly.

"Take a seat. Mia will join us shortly," Mr Blake greeted him in the dining room. The sheer height of the man would have proved enough to scare off any would-be suitor for his beautiful daughter, but, fortunately, he possessed the same easy-going countenance as Rory.

"Grab a couple of beers from the fridge, son." He ignored his wife's glower as they took their places at the formidable dining table.

With more glass and cutlery than Ikea's kitchen department, Caleb only relaxed when Rory passed him a cold bottle of beer.

"Cheers." He clinked his bottle to Caleb's and took a swig. Apparently the formal dining was optional.

Mia entered the room, wearing a knee-length white lace dress that left everything to Caleb's tawdry imagination, just as he took a swig of his drink.

"You all right?" Rory handed him a napkin as he spluttered beer all over the place.

"It must have gone down the wrong way." Caleb wiped the beer, or was it drool, from his chin and watched the ghost of a smile flit across Mia's face.

With exemplary etiquette she took her seat and sipped delicately from her water glass, her perfect poise making Caleb more uncomfortable than the whole dining showroom spread before him.

"So, Rory tells us you're leaving town soon," Mrs Blake interjected as they tucked into their seafood starter, making her opinion of his return very clear.

His bolshie personality immediately reared its head to piss her off. "Who knows? Thanks to Rory and Mia the house looks great and I don't have any immediate plans to go elsewhere." He shrugged, enjoying the reaction he gained around the table.

Good old Gayle held the stem of her crystal glass so tightly he waited for it to shatter, whilst Mr Blake's affable mood disappeared into a frown, and Mia's spoon stopped halfway to her open mouth. Only Rory took the news in his stride and carried on eating.

After that conversation-stopper, no one bothered to engage him in any further small talk and they reverted to discussing the inclement weather and declining economy amongst themselves throughout the remaining courses. Caleb tried to enjoy it for what it was—a home-cooked meal he didn't have to pay for.

The doorbell rang as dessert arrived. Mia's mother hurried to answer it as he attacked the elaborate spun sugar basket to get at the berries inside.

"Robert. How wonderful to see you." Whoever the new guest was, he certainly received a welcome Caleb could only dream of.

Mia, however, didn't appear to share her mother's enthusiasm. Her careful composure faltered as she leaned across the table to confront her father. "Dad? What is he doing here?"

He held his hands up in surrender, echoing her obvious surprise. "I have no idea."

Caleb watched the byplay in fascination as Robert entered the room. He didn't recognise the face but he did take an instant dislike to his smooth playboy looks. The suspiciously black hair, the beige slacks and pink polo shirt combo screamed pompous arse.

"Gayle mentioned you were having guests and I said I would pop in to say hello, sweetheart." He glided across the room to plant a kiss on Mia's cheek before making himself at home in the chair next to her.

"Hello, Robbie." The greeting was strained through gritted teeth. Caleb drew some satisfaction from the fact that she didn't return this tool's affection.

Mrs Blake rushed to pour a glass of the finest champagne for her favoured guest. Caleb took another swig from his bottle and eyeballed his new adversary, doubting Preppy ever lowered himself to drink common lager. He couldn't put his finger on why he had taken an instant dislike to this weed. Maybe it was the whiff of money and social standing, or perhaps he could blame it on the possessive air he took on around Mia.

Robbie laughed at some inane comment he had made himself, displaying rows of perfectly white, even teeth. He reached out to place his hand on Mia's arm, forcing Caleb to draw back his claws and fangs. Yes, his urge to punch this arsehole was definitely related to his pawing of Mia.

"Robert is partner in his father's property company. The Carson family is very well established in the area," Mrs Blake announced, most certainly for his benefit.

Whoop-de-frigging-do!

"Yeah? I would have thought a high-flyer like you would have wanted to start out on his own rather than hanging onto Daddy's coat tails," Caleb challenged him directly across the table.

Robbie took his time setting his glass down before he spoke. "And what is it you do?"

All eyes were on Caleb, waiting for him to humiliate himself. It seemed to be the theme of the evening and he'd had enough. Echoing Robbie's deliberate moves, he drained the last drop of beer and set the bottle on the table. "Well, you know I dropped out of school so I ain't got none of them there fancy qualifications. So, I have to use what the good Lord gave me."

He leant back in his chair until he balanced on the two back legs, and gestured between his legs. "What can I say? Rich housewives are only too happy to pay for a bit of rough."

He could practically feel the heat radiating from Mia's burning cheeks. Mr Blake spat beer all over the crisp, white linen tablecloth, while Rory laughed so hard it drowned out his mother's gasp of disgust. She sat at the head of the table, her eyes wide and her hand covering her mouth in absolute horror.

Rory scraped his chair back from the table and rose. "Thanks for dinner but I think I'll be on my way now."

With all ties to this shitty town now completely severed, he could think of nothing better than jumping on his bike and getting back on the road. For now, though, he would have to settle for kipping on the floor of the only place in town he couldn't be chased out of.

Making his way to the front door, it occurred to him that he might be better off living his life permanently as a wolf, with no one to piss him off and vice versa. As a wolf he could do what he did best. Survive.

The staccato beat of Mia's heels on the marble floor followed him down the corridor before he managed to escape the hell-hole. "What the hell was that all about?"

Anyone with a smidgeon of common sense would have kept walking out of that door and never looked back, but no one could ever accuse Caleb Jackson of acting any other way than impulsively.

"I am not here for either your amusement or your boyfriend's." The venom in that final word betrayed the twist of jealousy in his gut he had no right, and no wish, to feel. What was the point in carrying on this charade when she'd made it perfectly clear that she had no interest in him?

"I didn't ask you to come." She stopped chasing him.

He stopped running. "No, but you did kiss me."

"Shh!" She put her finger on her lips. "Get in there before someone hears you."

Unlocking a side door, she all but pushed him out of sight, thus underlining his position in her life. Books lined the room from floor to ceiling in the part of the house she introduced him to so unceremoniously. *Of course they have a library.*

Mia paced up and down, gesturing wildly. "I did. I did kiss you. I don't know why. I do know why. I wanted to."

"Doesn't lover boy know how to kiss?" He couldn't resist a dig. The bastard's nauseating scent still lingered on her.

"He's not my lover boy, or my boyfriend. Not anymore. And, for the record, yes, he is a crappy kisser." She stopped wearing the floorboards down long enough to indulge a smile.

This gorgeous woman deserved more than the cold fish he'd had the misfortune to meet tonight. It killed Caleb to imagine the two of them together, sure that the passion Mia exuded was solely reserved for him. She needed a reminder of why she enjoyed kissing him so much when it seemed to go against all her instincts.

He pinned her up against the stacks and staked his claim, crushing his mouth against hers. The yelp of her surprise was swallowed in the heat of the kiss, as he finally unleashed his pent-up desire from these past days of tiptoeing around the attraction.

Only intending to show her how good it could be with the right partner, he hadn't anticipated that his actions would take immediate effect. Or that the tables would be turned back on him. As she moulded her body and her lips to his, he couldn't imagine anyone else ever living up to Mia in the passion stakes.

If this should be their last time together, he didn't plan on questioning her change of heart, or looking deeper into his own feelings. Instead, he would erase Robbie from her memory, and make sure she found Caleb Jackson damn hard to forget.

He cupped her breast, taking the weight in his palm, and caressing the gradually hardening nipple through the lacy fabric of her dress. The brush of his thumb over that sensitive little nub brought his own flesh standing to attention, his jeans tightening until he was sure they would cut off the circulation to his dick.

It certainly drew Mia's interest as she moved her hands from his scalp to pull impatiently at his clothes. It set Caleb on fire to watch her work at the buttons on his fly, knowing that she wanted him, no matter how briefly. Encouraged by her assured moves, he slipped a hand under the hem of her dress and drew her panties down the smooth skin of her thighs. When he slid his fingers into her slick channel, the strength of her arousal was beyond doubt, and increasing his by the second.

He teased small circles around her clit, ignoring the dewy excitement glazing the tip of his penis to continue his Mia-focused quest. The clench and release of her inner muscles around his digits told him she was close and her knee, now hooked around his waist, enabled him to plunge deeper. Every 'mmm' and 'ahh' in his ear went some way to restoring his ego back to full health after its previous hit. The cry as she came, covering him in her juices, proved his final undoing.

With Mia every bit as horny as he, he grabbed a condom from his wallet and opened his fly. His erection sprang free, ready for action as he grabbed two handfuls of her sweet backside and hoisted her up around his hips.

One quick thrust took him home. Mia's tight, wet heat obliterated the last traces of doubt about her wanting him, and he branded her over and over again with every stroke of his cock. She was his, he was hers, and their bodies fitted so well together that it was impossible to tell where he ended and she began.

Mia braced herself against the bookcase, grabbing hold of a shelf as he drove into her hard, blinded by need. Books rained down around them as they rattled the stacks in their fervent union, but nothing could prevent them now from reaching their ultimate goal. The tomes kept crashing for as long as Caleb could keep up the pace and power of his rewarding hip thrusts.

The shallow breaths he panted out with every reconnection didn't come from the physical exertions, rather from the sheer strain of delaying his orgasm for as long as possible. But the yielding flesh of Mia's buttocks under his fingers, and the contrast of her constricting pussy around his staff, conspired to undo his good intentions. It only took a nip at the crook of his neck, courtesy of his lover's overzealous lips, to finally send him tumbling into a state of ecstasy.

As he came with a satisfied growl, Mia ground her pelvis to his and fucked him right back until she reached her second climax of the evening. The sweet and spicy aspects of her personality would never cease to amaze him, or turn him on.

He withdrew slowly from her slippery grasp and let her slide down his body until she stood back on solid ground. When he let her go in order to remove the evidence of their liaison from the end of his dick, she almost fell to the floor, her legs as shaky as his.

For some reason she wouldn't look him in the eye. Another attack of social guilt he assumed, once she'd satisfied her carnal urges and remembered he was merely a peasant come calling at the big house. Watching her retrieve her panties at his feet pissed all over the idea of her in that ivory tower, so far out of his reach. He took some pleasure in her discomfort, but not enough to compensate for the snub.

"I might not be much of a dinner guest but I sure know how to fuck." Caleb buttoned up his jeans, and his dignity, and walked away.

On unsteady legs Mia made her way back to the dining room, only going as far as the doorway. "I'm not feeling very well. I'm going to bed."

Refusing to give those present any time to quiz her, she left before they smelt Caleb's scent on her. Inside and out. They could discuss his outlandish behaviour and her mother's decision to invite her ex to the house when she could think more clearly. Right now her head whirled with confusion.

She stumbled into her bedroom and locked the door behind her, shedding her clothes on her way to the en suite bathroom. Naked and shivering she flipped on the shower and stood beneath its cleansing stream.

The warm water soothed the slight ache between her thighs where Caleb had sought her so ravenously, bringing them both so quickly to climax. The skin on her butt cheeks stung where his nails had dug into her flesh, joining their bodies together so completely. Every niggle of pain refused to let her forget the passion he had stirred in her. Even now, her sex swelled as she thought of his hot and heavy breath on her face, her body caged beneath him, and it made the tug of longing in her loins too much to ignore.

Mia let her hand travel between her legs to investigate her own arousal and dipped one digit into her irresistibly wet entrance. Retracing Caleb's journey, she delved deep into the silken folds to explore her desires. She imagined him there with her, inside her, calling her to orgasm at her own hand.

The cascade of water from above carried away all the evidence, and, as the shower wrapped her in its warm embrace, she let her tears flow freely. There was no chance of winning back her parents' trust and respect if she insisted on acting like a common little slut. *How can one man make me feel so good about myself and so bad at the same time?*

But she couldn't refute the effect he had on her body, even if she wanted to. The addictive nature of discovering her sexuality she likened to waking up in a new world, where she had so much to catch up on. Not once in the years she'd spent with Robbie had she experienced what every other sexually active woman took for granted—that connection with her partner, that feeling of desirability, and, most importantly of all, enjoyment. Now that Caleb was there to provide her with those missing elements it frightened her.

Her parents would never approve. She wasn't sure that she did. He was coarse, unrefined and unreliable. Everything Robbie wasn't. But there was no question how Caleb felt about her when she saw that passion in every look, every move he made. With Robbie, she suspected she was nothing more than a convenience at times. Yet she'd stayed with him much longer than was good for her, simply to keep her parents happy.

Logically, other than enjoying the sins of each other's flesh, she knew she had done no wrong with Caleb. The tiresome worries came entirely from her quarter. Trapped by her own fear, she let those around her dictate how they thought she should behave.

Weary from the day's physical and emotional labours, she shut off the water and climbed into bed. It didn't matter that her skin and hair were still wet, she just wanted sleep to claim her and put an end to her anxieties.

The last thought she had on the subject as her head hit the pillow, was that someday soon she would have to grow a pair and find the courage to live her life the way she wanted to. If only she knew what that was.

Chapter Four

Mia tossed and turned, her restless legs making short work of the carefully tucked bed covers. Too hot, too cold, she couldn't get comfortable, and she held Caleb Jackson entirely responsible.

After twenty-four very long hours, her body cried out for the comfort of his touch, ached for that sense of completion only he could provide. She wondered what spell he had cast over her to make her crave him even more than chocolate. *Mmm, chocolate-dipped Caleb...*

"Aagh!" She cast off the last of the sheets in exasperation. This self-imposed torture might end up doing more harm than succumbing to her desires. If her levels of horniness increased any further, she feared she would jump on the first eligible bachelor to cross her path. It made much more sense to capitulate to the very man who had caused her condition in the first place. A day spent with her conscience and libido vying for control had finally been won out by her new bestie.

As her parents slept soundly on the floor above, Mia crept through the house. The absurdity of a grown woman sneaking out for a booty call wasn't lost on her. Especially when she hadn't rebelled once in her teens, and had saved herself for Robbie of all people.

The front door clicked behind her, and she ran barefoot across the lawn, tossing her nightdress asunder to transform into her wolf. The scent of her grey wolf hung in the air around the woods. He had been there recently. *Watching me?* Perhaps his wounded pride had also been beaten into submission by animal lust. In that case she might not have to grovel too much to seek his help out with her predicament.

With renewed enthusiasm, she raced on through the trees, over the hills, in pursuit of her mate. The trail took her directly towards the cottage, its faint light burning through the darkness. She should have known Caleb would rather hole up in discomfort there before he would back down and ask her brother for another night's lodging.

As she approached the house, she reassumed her human form. The cool air prickled her skin and puckered her nipples, but thankfully she found the door unlocked. This was not a man used to the practicalities of home security.

The inside of the house didn't provide much more heat than outside, but the sight of Caleb curled up on the floor soon warmed her. She envied his peaceful sleep, even though he lay on the hard wood floor fully dressed, using his jacket for a pillow.

Seduction didn't come easy to a girl more used to Robbie's wham-bam-get-your-coat technique. The longer she stood there completely starkers, the more doubts crept in. It had all seemed so easy from the comfort of her bed — get laid, keep it secret, everyone's a winner. Now in the harsh fluorescent light she wondered if he would even want her. Maybe their last bout of sexual gymnastics at the house had been his swan song before he moved on. His parting words certainly hadn't held a hint of sentimentality, or indicated an interest in seeing her again. After everyone's behaviour that night he was well within his rights to tell her to go to hell, but she was here now.

Pulling on her metaphoric big girl pants, Mia shook off her personal demons and lay down beside him. She brushed away the dark blond locks falling across his eyes, her touch dragging him back to semi-consciousness. Caleb wrinkled his nose, and she leaned in to kiss his slightly parted lips. When he didn't respond, she traced the tip of her tongue across his bottom lip. He murmured and turned further onto his side, throwing an arm across her hip.

The apparent power she held over his sleeping form proved impossible to ignore. Without his smart remarks and swagger that reduced her to a submissive mess, she was free to do a little tormenting of her own. A gentle blow in his ear provoked him until an agitated hand batted her away. The barely-there kisses pressed into the base of his neck produced a whimper. When she popped open his fly for what she really wanted, he clamped his large hand painfully around her wrist.

"What are you doing?" No trace of her jovial mood reflected in the fiery amber eyes now staring back at her.

She tried to distract him with a series of open-mouthed kisses placed along his jaw line, but he shrank away.

"Only last night you were embarrassed to have me in your house, and now you're in mine? Naked?" *It had taken him long enough to notice.*

"Are you complaining?" As his grip slackened, she renewed her bold advance to take hold of his rapidly growing erection. He could protest all he wanted, but his body told a different story.

"No. But why am I suddenly flavour of the month again?" He shifted uncomfortably, but Mia persisted in stroking the full length of his silky shaft. "You are driving me crazy, Ms Blake."

"It occurred to me that I am running from something we both want very much." She nibbled on his earlobe and sucked it into her mouth, determined that he should follow her lead and overlook all the whys and wherefores.

His Adam's apple bobbed as he swallowed hard. "What's that?"

"No strings sex," she whispered into his ear.

His cock jerked its appreciation but his eyes remained unsure. "That's what you want?"

"Yes. Unless I'm expected to pay for your services too?" Undoubtedly she would empty her entire bank account for a night with him, but she couldn't pass up the opportunity to tease.

Caleb covered his face with his hands and groaned. "I'm trying to forget I said that."

Mia let loose with a giggle, remembering her mother's horror. "So, you're not the highly sought-after stud you claimed to be? How disappointing."

That cheeky grin she'd worried might not make an appearance finally spread across his face as her good mood started to work its magic.

"I didn't say that. I just don't accept payment for my skills."

"Good, because what I have in mind for you while you're in town would probably drive me to bankruptcy." Even simply thinking about what they could get up to with her inhibitions under lock and key for the time being sent butterflies dive-bombing in the pit of her stomach. Like one of those corkscrew rollercoasters at the funfair, Caleb scared and excited her. There were ups and downs, moments when she'd scream or wait with baited breath for the next sudden move, but in the end she'd finish the ride with a great big smile on her face.

The hearty rumble of his laugh brought back the easy camaraderie she so enjoyed with him. "Why don't you show me what you have in mind?"

Eyes dark with desire challenged her and she was more than happy to oblige. With a sharp tug, the restrictions of his trousers and underwear were no more. He was definitely happy to see her. Again, she teased his bottom lip with her tongue whilst running her thumb back and forth over the tip of his penis. The double action made him buck beneath her, until she shimmied down his body to focus on the part of him straining for release.

"Mmm." She savoured him slowly, as though he boasted a candy-covered cock, and she had a very sweet tooth. The velvety skin and the rigid flesh grasped in her hand were treated with reverence from their devoted follower.

She licked circles around and around the swollen purple head, washed over the tip to lap up the first drops of his excitement, and took him fully into her mouth. While cupping and squeezing his sac, she sucked on his length, from the base to the tip, and repeated until her jaw ached. Even when she had freed him from his oral restraints she didn't let up the pressure, merely captured his erection in her firm hand instead.

While she worked his shaft at a steady pace, she playfully nuzzled and kissed his balls, straying south just enough to gain a reaction.

"Fucking hell! That feels amazing." His colourful verbal response did wonders for her self-esteem, but also intensified her reasons for coming to him. At least on this occasion she had Caleb on hand to relieve her symptoms.

They worked together to tug off the rest of his clothes and slip on a condom, leaving him delightfully naked for her to straddle. The strong muscles between her thighs reminded her of the horse she had ridden many years ago, a wild, powerful beast. With any luck she could tame this stallion as easily as her first love, and ride him just as hard.

Mia sighed when the blunt head of his erection parted her folds to forge her and Caleb together. The thick fill of him guided her to that selfish slice of heaven where no thoughts dared enter, and her libido governed her entire body. Steeling the palms of her hands on the tic-tac-toe board of his abs, she moved quickly up and down his pleasure-giving, fleshy staff.

"Hey, wait for me!" Caleb pinched her nipples between his fingers to bring her spiralling back from the brink. Keeping her pinned to him, he sat up and kissed her with a grounding passion to slow her pace. The sensations of his tongue in her mouth and his cock in her hole at the same time overwhelmed her, priming every nerve ending for an enjoyable finale.

He set a steady rhythm and lay back down, bringing her with him so they were chest to chest. No words were needed to communicate his desires as he let his body do the talking. His hands gripped her hips and, regardless of her powerful position, he took control and dictated the pace — quick, quick, slow. A delicious tango.

He stoked the fire he'd lit inside her from their very first encounter until it raged out of control. She anticipated each arch of his pelvis, meeting him with increased hunger at every bump and grind. That wonderful pressure building inside her, which she was getting way too used to, started in her toes, steadily rising to creep along her inner thigh, and concentrate in her tightening pussy.

With help she flew into the clouds, piloted by the one person who seemed to know who she was and what she needed, even when she didn't. The force of her climax surprised her as she broke apart, zapping her of all energy to the point of collapse.

Caleb flipped an orgasmically-dazed Mia over onto her back and took charge of his own release. The feral growl that vibrated through his body when he came sent quivers of delight into hers with the knowledge that he was just as out of control around her. Surely he couldn't turn down her proposal with this feeling to look forward to wherever, and whenever, they wanted?

When the final tremors of his orgasm subsided, he lay down beside her. It seemed right when he held her in his arms, the two of them spooning like any other couple would after making love. If life ever played fair, one day she could have it all.

* * * *

Flickers of daylight reached behind Caleb's closed lids to coax him awake. Mia stirred beside him, giving a stretch that showcased everything she had to offer. It hadn't been a dream?

"What time is it?" She yawned and cuddled back into his side.

"Dunno." Quite happy to lie there all day long, he neither knew nor cared about the time. He settled down for another doze, but Mia tensed beside him.

She sat up, hugging her arms around her knees. "I have to go."

As always, her panic pricked their bubble, to turn the dream to dust.

"So, this is another regret-filled parting of the ways?" Some men would probably be grateful for the quick getaway, and usually he was one of those men. For some reason, each snub from Mia cut that much more deeply. Yet, the masochist in him couldn't resist any chance to be with her.

"I have to carry on like this never happened? Again?" For once it would be nice to have someone act proud of their association with him instead of showing shame.

Mia frowned at him. "I thought we agreed on the 'no strings' thing?"

He frowned right back. "But you're still sneaking out."

A quick smile unfurled her brow, and she leaned over to kiss him softly on the mouth. "I am not sneaking out. I am sneaking back into my house. In case you haven't noticed, I am naked. Besides, if this is nothing more than a bit of fun, there is no reason to get my family involved. They don't need to know my every move."

"And, girl, you have some moves." The wink he gave her gained him a playful slap to the arm, while he did his best to ignore the slight against him as her guilty little secret.

"I'm serious. I want to enjoy this for what it is, and not worry what other people think of me." Her honesty came with a bite. That notion that he wasn't good enough to parade on her arm resonated with a heavy clang.

But surely he wanted the same thing—sex with Mia, no commitment, and absolutely no reason to cross paths with the Wicked Bitch of the West up at Blake Towers.

"I'm going now before anyone spots me roaming naked in the hills and asks any questions. Okay?" She patted his hand the same way he did when letting a girl down after a one-night stand.

"Okay." He stifled a laugh at the sudden role reversal, not sure he would feel more emasculated if he grew a pair of tits.

They parted on the doorstep with a lingering kiss that said everything of the times they could look forward to. With no definite plans for when they would meet up again he feared he'd be left there pining until she could snatch five minutes unsupervised to slink back. He needed to find something to occupy his time there in between visits, for the sake of his sanity, and his reputation.

As Mia changed into her stunning white wolf and disappeared into the trees, Caleb wondered when exactly she had become such a big part of his life.

* * * *

The water swirled, white foam bobbing on the surface as he rinsed the razor in the sink. When he leaned in to check his reflection, it finally dawned on him that this was all his—the sink, the mirror, the bathroom, the house—all of it.

With a shake of his head he fished the plug out from the sink and let the soapy water drain away. Up until now he could have fitted all of his worldly possessions onto the back of his motorbike, and now… He reached for the towel to pat his face dry and took a good look out of the window at the rolling fields he currently possessed.

Maybe as a landowner now he needed to buy some tweeds and a shotgun as opposed to the ripped jeans and smile he currently sported. Content with all that he surveyed, he didn't even resent the huge slice of the property sold off over the years to fund his father's excesses.

Once upon a time their ancestors had owned the majority of the farmland hereabouts, and the Jackson name had demanded respect. A certain responsibility lay with him now, as the last member of the clan. The line finished with him, and there was a possibility that he could be the one to blame for wiping them from Olcan Hills' future history. After all, the chances of him settling down with a loving wife to have fat wolfie babies were slim to say the least.

The walls of guilt closed in on him and the urge to run became overwhelming.

The last clean T-shirt he owned, a freebie courtesy of some beer promotion, lay in a ball at the bottom of his rucksack. He pulled it on along with his black leather jacket and boots, opting for the human method of escape today.

* * * *

He cruised the country roads on his beloved Triumph Thunderbird Storm, thankful for the sacrifices he'd made to purchase his dream motorcycle. Every double shift, late night gig and not knowing where he would sleep from one day to the next was worth it for this adrenaline rush.

Exhilaration fuelled his journey as he wound his way through the hills, twisting and turning as the wind carried away his problems. He didn't set out with a destination in mind, but he slowed the bike when he came across the local cemetery. He'd never made it to his father's funeral. After all, he wasn't a hypocrite.

The man had bullied and beaten every ounce of love out of Caleb until he hadn't even been able to find it in him to mourn the loss. Yet, here he stood at the graveside of the only parent he'd ever known. The black marble headstone, no doubt provided by the good people of Olcan Hills, looked stately. Something the great John Jackson would surely have approved of. But to Caleb it was simply another symbol of the lies.

"'A great man', huh?" The gold lettering told of a person whom Caleb didn't recognise. "I wish I had come sooner. To tell you, tell them, what a cruel bastard you were behind closed doors. But who would have believed me anyway when you were such a convincing saint to the rest of the world?"

No one could have known that the late, great John Jackson had taken out all his frustrations on his only son, when he portrayed himself as a man who would do anything for anyone. Even thinking about him increased Caleb's resentment to the point that it left a hollow crater where his heart should be.

His thoughts drifted to Mia, as if she was his body's natural attempt to repair the trauma inflicted by his father. Alcohol usually did the same trick, but she definitely seemed like the best cure-all for his ills. Better than that, he could have Mia and beer at the same time. Screw waiting around for her to come to him, he knew exactly where he wanted to spend the next few hours.

* * * *

With a smile for everyone and a gentle laugh that he could pick out across the busy pub, even just to watch her move behind the bar soothed his troubled soul. Instead of the frosty air she often took on when confronted with him in public, she gave him a friendly wave when she spotted him.

Only the pink tinge to her complexion gave away any clue that their relationship went beyond mere acquaintances. The shared secret made him stand taller in the room full of judgemental arseholes who believed that he'd wronged his father in so many ways. This wonderful woman was his. For now, at least.

"Hey, Mia." He sauntered over to the bar, resisting the strong urge to kiss, or even touch her when he knew the slightest contact would end in him ravishing her on the bar top.

"A beer please, barmaid." Picturing her in a wench outfit, her bosom heaving from lacy white ruffles, didn't help the growing discomfort in his pants. One sniff of this hot she-wolf and he reverted to the horny leg-humping mutt everyone assumed him to be.

"Would you like me to top that up with lemonade?" She nodded towards Rory parked at the end of the bar.

Sheesh! Does this guy actually have a life of his own?

"I suppose you'd better make it a shandy since I'm driving. I don't want a run-in with the law, now, do I?" With his need for alcohol already overshadowed by Mia's more intoxicating presence, a sip of the now innocuous drink slaked his thirst.

As Mia returned to serve her other customers, Caleb found himself gravitating towards Rory. Strangely, since his return to the Hills, languishing in his own company no longer held the same appeal it once did.

"Do you want to slap the cuffs on me now?" Caleb held out his wrists with some apprehension. The Blake family exhibited such changeable personalities that he couldn't predict how Rory would react to him after the disastrous dinner.

He patted the seat next to him. Definitely preferable to the headlock Caleb had envisaged. "Personally, I enjoyed the entertainment, but I think mother is still recovering from the shock of having a gigolo at the dinner table."

"Jesus! I was joking!" If word got around that he made his living fucking rich housewives, he could kiss goodbye to any local goodwill that might have remained.

"I know, but where the fuck did that come from?" To Caleb's relief, Rory laughed and displayed no signs of anger in his direction.

Caleb exhaled the breath his lungs had refused to let go of since he'd approached Mia's brother. "I don't know. I guess I let my temper get the better of me when Robbie had a go at me in front of everyone. Please pass on my apologies."

"No worries. I'm not exactly a fan of his either, and Mum can be full-on at times too. I'm sure she'll get over it. Once she's disinfected everything you've touched, of course." They exchanged grins, and Caleb could only imagine what means of capital punishment they would inflict on him if they knew he'd touched every inch of Mia.

"Do I take it I'm off the guest list for Gayle's next soirée?" At least half of the family didn't appear to hold Caleb's bad temper against him. The half whose opinion he cared about.

Isn't that strange? Now that Mia and I are together, having Rory on side suddenly matters. Maybe it's because her brother holds so much sway with her, or possibly because I know he could beat the shit outta me if he felt so inclined.

"Well, I'd hold off on ordering the tux for now. If it's any consolation, the dinner parties are full of boring tossers like Robbie Carson. I prefer to socialise with more…interesting people. Here's to raising a little hell now and then." Rory raised his coffee cup in salute and Caleb clinked his glass to it.

"To hellions!" *Let's hope you still feel the same way when you find out your sister has crossed over into the dark side.*

Chapter Five

Mia couldn't wait to finish her shift. Especially with Caleb here to drive her to distraction. Watching her secret lover laughing and joking with her big brother caused no end of conflicting emotions. On one hand, fear lingered that he would find out about their shenanigans, and about the trouble it could lead to with her family. But to see them getting on so well together also played a merry tune on her heartstrings.

The what-ifs ran amok, teasing her about how life could be with both men in her life. If Caleb could be the man she needed him to be, if Rory backed off just enough to let her breathe, life would be perfect. In the end, though, Caleb wouldn't stay and her parents would never accept him anyway. For now, she would simply have to settle for the fantastic sex. That thought was incentive enough to get her through the working day.

Her shift took an unexpected turn when Naomi took a phone call a while later.

"What's up?" Mia could see the worry etched on her face as soon as she hung up the telephone.

Naomi checked her watch for the umpteenth time. Something had clearly rattled the usually unflappable Miss Doyle. "That was Emily's nursery. She's complaining of a sore tummy, so I need to go pick her up. The trouble is the nursery is forty minutes away."

"I can cover until you get back. I'm sure I can manage the afternoon rush of soup and sandwiches." Even if the orders backed up she was sure she could sweet-talk the two men hovering around her like flies into helping.

Naomi wrinkled her nose and the offer fell flat. "I have deliveries coming I need to sign for. Even if I do go get her, what the hell am I going to do with her this afternoon?" The rubbing of her temples predicted a migraine that really would leave Mia in the lurch.

A strong independent woman, Naomi managed her role of single mother as efficiently as her position as owner of The Wild Dog. She wouldn't relinquish control of either without a fight, and she'd made it clear in the past that she had no family to call on for help.

"Maybe we could tuck her up in the back room?" Mia didn't relish the idea of adding clearing out the room to her list of things to do, but if they didn't sort something out soon she would never get to spend quality time with Caleb.

"I could go and pick her up." Rory's bolt-from-the-blue offer shocked them all into silence. Tumbleweeds blew across the floor as they gawped at him open-mouthed. He was the last person Mia had expected to volunteer.

When no one reacted verbally, Rory's shoulders dropped and he mumbled into his coffee, "I was only trying to help. I'm not a complete stranger to Emily, and, well, I thought you could use the time to get your deliveries organised."

Naomi blinked furiously and opened and closed her mouth several times before she finally spoke. "Thank you, Rory. That would be great. I'll phone ahead and let the nursery know you're coming."

A double-bumper surprise on top of Rory's bombshell, to think she would even let him assume responsibility for her precious baby.

Whilst Rory looked as though he'd won the lottery, Naomi floated past Mia in some sort of daze. It amazed her how one act of kindness could melt the ice around the most hardened of hearts. And she hadn't even had to interfere.

Caleb, too, picked up on the vibes after Rory had left with Naomi's gratitude ringing through the premises. "If we can prise Velcro man from your side and reattach him to the boss lady, maybe we'll get some peace."

Mia collected the empty glasses lining the bar and winked at him. "My thoughts exactly."

Ultimately denied Caleb as a permanent feature in her bed, she would make do with number two on her wish list — some time out from big bro so she could get jiggy without worrying about her grey wolf-shaped secret being discovered any time soon.

Now why won't that clock go any frigging faster so I can get the hell out of here?

* * * *

Rory returned after the lunchtime feeding frenzy, but before the delivery showed up. He cut quite a figure on his entrance, a towering giant carrying a tiny infant in one arm.

Naomi appeared in an instant to fuss around Emily. "Thanks again, Rory. How is she?"

"She's running a slight temperature and she's a bit, er, clingy." He attempted to extricate the chubby arms from around his neck, but she tightened her hold and buried her head in his chest. No wonder. Mia remembered how safe and protected her brother had made her feel when she was young enough to appreciate it.

"Now, Emily. Let Mr Blake go. He has work to do." Naomi tried to persuade her to let go, but Emily shook her dark curly head and pouted, displaying the same stubbornness as her mother.

"It's okay. I'm off on leave at the minute. I can take her back with me until you're finished here if you want? I think I've finally figured out the mechanics of the dreaded car seat." Mia thought Naomi might faint on the spot as Rory rode in on his white charger for a second time.

Instead, she stroked Emily's forehead and kissed her flushed cheek. "I don't want to put you to any trouble, Rory. I'll collect her as soon as this blasted stock arrives."

"It's no trouble at all. Besides, I don't think my cling-on here is going anywhere soon." He let go of his charge, her grip so tight she didn't move even without his support.

"Okay, but phone me if there is any change in her." Naomi didn't sound one hundred per cent convinced and Mia stepped in to reassure her that she was doing the right thing.

"Don't worry. Rory practically raised me. He's more than capable of watching her for a few hours." The watery look she received in return told of Naomi's struggle with her inner control freak to believe her.

"Look, as soon as this blasted delivery comes you can take off. We'll get one of the evening staff in early for some overtime." This time Naomi managed a wobbly smile. It unnerved Naomi to see her so vulnerable. She prayed the lorry would turn up soon before she witnessed a complete mummy melt-down, and Mia was left holding everything together.

* * * *

The way the day had gone so far, it came as no surprise that the driver chose today to make The Dog the last stop on his round. Mia surmised that only Rory's constant updates on Emily's condition stopped Naomi from tearing the driver to shreds when he arrived ten minutes before the end of the shift. As it was, her glare sent him scurrying to the back of the truck to unload his cargo and make a quick getaway.

"Some of us have more important things to do than wait around until you decide to grace us with your presence." Naomi signed off on the order with a vicious swipe of her pen that made Mia wince. She knew there was a reason that she stayed on the woman's right side.

"I'm out of here." Naomi tugged on her coat as she walked to the door, her relief obvious. Then she added, "I suggest you get going too before another catastrophe rears its ugly head to scupper your plans." She threw a knowing glance in Caleb's direction.

"I'm sure I don't know what you mean." Mia practically pushed her out through the heavy doors.

"Come off it. I'm not stupid. He's sat here all afternoon nursing soft drinks, and I don't think he's here for the ambience."

At that moment Caleb slipped Mia one of his sexy grins and rendered her attempts to feign ignorance futile.

"You're young. Go have some fun." Sounding wise beyond her thirty or so years, Naomi left her with a friendly hug.

"For God's sake tell me we can go now. As much as I love you, er, love being with you, I could do with getting away from here." Caleb forced her to do a double take.

Regardless that he'd tried to cover up and had leapt like a scalded cat from his chair, she couldn't erase the words from her memory.

'I love you.'

Words she had never expected to hear from him. Words she didn't know what to do with.

Fuck! Neither the air blasting around him, nor the warmth of Mia's arms wrapped around his waist could make him forget his latest fuck-up.

'I love you.'

He'd never said the words in his life, had never heard them, and had never known what they meant. Until now? He didn't know.

Perhaps the old place made him more sentimental than he cared to admit, or maybe an afternoon spent watching this beautiful creature had bewitched him into saying it. To her credit she didn't pounce on the declaration like some needy women might have. Then again, she could have resented the fact that he'd said it as much as he did.

It would take more than the short ride home on the bike to figure out what the hell it all meant. When they stopped outside his house, he had only one thing on his mind.

"I can't wait to get you inside." He helped her off the bike, eager to show rather than tell her how he felt about her.

"Why? What do you have planned? A candlelit dinner for two? Or a movie and takeout?" She unzipped his jacket and trailed a finger down the front of his shirt.

"Shit. I thought we could just shag. But if you'd prefer something else…"

"No. That'll do for starters." Giggling like a schoolgirl, Mia grabbed his hand and hurried to the house with Caleb nibbling her neck as she opened the door. She tasted sweet on his tongue, and, impatient to feast on the rest of her body, Caleb unbuttoned her shirt as they stepped inside.

"Caleb?"

"Hmm?" He slid his hands under the satin cups of her bra and took her weighty globes in his hands.

"Caleb, I think someone's been here." The panicky tone ripped him from his erotic travels and opened his eyes to the fresh horror.

"What the fuck?" Plaster and paint lay in chunks at their feet, the interior walls of his house peppered with holes. It looked as though they'd had a run-in with a sledgehammer.

The mood well and truly ruined, he left Mia to fix her clothes. "Stay here in case there's anyone still inside."

He moved with caution to investigate but the house was as empty as he'd left it that morning. Only now with added ventilation.

"Oh God. Caleb." Mia's anguished wail followed him down the hall, ignoring his warning. He didn't waste his breath scolding her. This woman's forceful will was one of the many things he loved about her. Liked. Liked about her.

She walked through the house after him, trailing her fingers across every ding and dent in their path as if touching the evidence to make sure it was real. He couldn't quite believe it himself. The doors he and Rory had hung only yesterday were battered and smashed with whatever weapon had also smashed up the bathroom. The sink where he'd washed only hours ago now lay smashed—shards of white porcelain scattered on the floor.

"Who would do this? Why would they do this?" Mia wandered into the bedroom where fresh graffiti stained the walls. The elusive ninja vandal had cleverly improvised with yesterday's leftover paint and thrown it aimlessly round the room. The white gloss smeared her fingertip as she reached out to touch it.

"I have no idea." The knot in his stomach pulled tighter with every new discovery. Not only at the personal trauma of finding his home ransacked for a second time, but also in despair of all the hard work lost.

Where he could pass off the first spate as a random act, this latest episode was a direct personal attack on him. Surely, apart from Mia's parents, he hadn't been in town long enough to piss off anyone to this extent? The very idea of Gayle Blake storming through the house in a ball gown wreaking havoc with a sledgehammer managed to lift his dark mood a fraction.

"I didn't lock the front door." It didn't explain the vendetta against him, or his sink, but some of the responsibility rested on his shoulders. By accepting that, he hoped to take away some of the worry clouding the brilliance of her blue eyes.

"What will you do?" Poor Mia looked heartbroken on his behalf.

"What can I do, except start again from scratch? And start locking that bloody front door." The daunting prospect of his workload took second place to his growing paranoia. How far would this stalker go to get at him?

Caleb's calmness bothered Mia, as if having people smash up his shit was an everyday occurrence for him. Maybe it was. *What do I really know about him?* She hadn't bothered to find out anything about him beyond his considerable talents in the bedroom. For all she knew, he could be involved in all manner of dodgy dealings with the sort of people who liked to express themselves through the medium of a sledgehammer.

A shudder ripped through her at the thought of Caleb at the mercy of this hammer-wielding maniac. Forgetting her earlier plea for independence, Mia's first instinct about the whole situation was to run to her big brother for help. "You need to report this to the police."

Caleb's emphatic "No" did nothing to ease her fears or suspicions.

"Why on earth not?"

He lifted the upturned tin of paint from the floor and began to mop up the spillage with a rag, making no attempt to preserve the scene. "Look, I don't want any trouble. Even if someone is literally intent on bringing it to my door. Right now, that shitty offer I got for the place doesn't seem so bad. I could add a 'sold as seen' clause and get the fuck out of here."

He dumped the paint-sodden rag in the bin with excessive force. Perhaps Mr Cool wasn't entirely as laid-back as she'd first thought. But she didn't want him to wave the white flag and run away. If he did, he might never come back.

"We should go see Rory." He could talk some sense into Caleb. Mia had her own selfish reasons for not wanting Caleb to leave, but her brother wouldn't let the sheer injustice of the situation pass without a fight either.

"Can we leave your fucking brother out of this just for once?" Caleb punched the door, adding to the structural woes of the property, before he stomped off.

"Hey!" Mia took off after him, pissed off by the completely unnecessary act. She grabbed him by the shoulder and spun him around with a surprising show of strength. "Take it out on the people who deserve it."

Under her palm, the coiled muscles slackened. "Sorry. When I think of all the trouble he went to, getting everyone here to patch the place up... I don't want to go cap in hand again. I'll sort this."

"There's no need to be so proud. Or stubborn." She waited for him to throw that particular character trait back in her face, but he was too caught up in playing the martyr to notice.

"Maybe I'm sick of Super Rory swooping in to save the day and making me feel like the village idiot." Just when she'd thought they were making progress, Caleb's defences had shot up again, topped with some barbed wire to make sure no one got close.

"You are a fucking idiot!" That did it. Caleb stopped slouching and snapped upright. Mia gulped, but she didn't want another whiny Robbie clone. *Bring back my kick-ass bad boy.*

"You need to find out who's doing this and put a stop to it. Or I will." She folded her arms across her chest, drawing on her inner warrior princess. It merely succeeded in making him smirk.

"Yes, mistress." The spark flared back to life in Caleb's green eyes, and he pulled her into a confident, assured kiss. His attempt to take her mind off the subject may have worked temporarily, but his safety wasn't something she would leave to chance.

Chapter Six

Mia preferred Rory's house to the one she shared with her parents. Much like its owner, the modest dwelling didn't pretend to be anything other than a solid dependable structure. It didn't need fancy embellishments to be loved.

She let herself in with her own key. Rory understood her need to escape from her parents on a regular basis, and let her veg out here when she needed to.

"Come on, huff muffin." With the door held open, she hurried Caleb inside.

He rolled his eyes at her, but swallowed his pride to enter the house. In her heart she hoped he'd agreed to come, not simply to pacify her, but because deep down he knew he could confide in Rory.

She couldn't get her head around his resentment that festered towards her brother. Yes, they were close, but Caleb certainly had no reason to be jealous. The two men were similar in so many ways — both independent, pig-headed, dominant males who played huge roles in her life. If not for Caleb's sake, for her own selfish reasons, she wished they could happily co-exist. After all, she would rely on Rory's steadfast support when Caleb inevitably left her.

"Hi, bro." Seeing him on the settee, fire blazing in the hearth beside him, brought comfort, even as she imagined life without Caleb.

"Hey, sis. Caleb." Rory didn't get up. He couldn't with Emily curled up into a ball on his lap. Mia thought the protective father look rather suited him.

Naomi entered carrying steaming mugs of coffee to complete the cosy scene. "Oh, hi, you two. Little Miss Cranky is refusing point blank to leave Rory's side."

Neither Naomi nor Rory appeared too distressed over the matter. In fact, they looked every inch the happy family together—a sight that wouldn't have been out of place on a cheesy Christmas card.

Rather than make some flippant comment that would unsettle the oblivious couple, Mia made herself at home in one of the comfy seats and urged Caleb to do the same.

He took it upon himself to disrupt the easy atmosphere with the real reason they were here. "I've had another break-in at the cottage."

Rory automatically morphed from the laid-back family man into the vigilant police officer. "Did they take anything?"

"There's nothing left to take." Caleb snorted but failed to disguise the hurt in his voice. "They smashed the place up pretty good."

Rory plucked Emily from his person and handed the sleeping bundle to her mother. "When?"

"Sometime today while I was out."

Waiting on me.

"In broad daylight?" Rory scowled as Caleb nodded. "Someone's obviously watching your every move.

Someone who's trying to send you a message. Any idea what that could be?"

Caleb didn't shy away from the blunt line of questioning. "Rory, I haven't seen anyone here in eleven years. I have no idea who's doing this. If it's one of the locals holding a grudge from something I did when I was a kid, surely they'd want me to leave town as soon as possible? Not screw up my chances of a quick sale."

Mia braved a suggestion, "What about your father? Is it possible someone is taking their anger out on you over something he did?"

Both men looked at her with puzzled expressions but for very different reasons. Rory couldn't understand why she would besmirch their past alpha's character, and Caleb couldn't know how much insight she had into his father's true nature. Witnessing the brutal beating John Jackson had dealt his son was a secret she had kept for many years. It gave her some understanding of Caleb's strained relationships with those around him, and also made her question what else his old man had got up to behind closed doors.

"I don't think he made many enemies, outside of his own family." A shutter came down over his features with the mere mention of his father. Obviously it wasn't a matter up for discussion and Mia immediately sensed that she should back away from the subject. For a proud man like Caleb, any hint that she had seen him at his most vulnerable might shatter their fragile relationship.

"I'd like to take a look at the damage. Do you want me to call it in?" Rory got to his feet, raring to go.

Caleb stopped him. "I don't mind you coming over, but I don't want anyone else."

Rory didn't argue and the two left in companionable silence. They understood each other on a level neither of them appreciated. Mia wanted to bang their heads together.

"Are you okay?" Naomi, quiet during the discussion, now approached, carrying her babe in her arms.

"Yeah. Just upset for Caleb. Anyway, do you want to put her down in the bedroom rather than take her back out into the cold?" Spots of red bloomed on Emily's cheeks. Guilt would have eaten Mia alive to send her out into the frosty air.

"Do you think Rory would mind?" Naomi shifted the dead weight from one arm to the other, looking as exhausted as her daughter.

"Not at all. Put her down in the back bedroom and I'll put the kettle on for another cuppa." She could do with the break—dealing with all this emotion and testosterone was exhausting.

* * * *

It didn't take long to survey the damage. It lay at their feet in plain sight. Rory wore the same serious expression as he had done the first time around.

"You're staying at mine tonight." He was probably used to barking out orders, but Caleb sure as hell wasn't used to following them.

"No."

"Yes."

"You're not my alpha." This lone wolf belonged to no pack.

"No, but I do want my sister safe."

Shit! Caleb could tell by the steely gaze pinning him to the spot that Rory knew exactly what they'd been up to in the cottage. He didn't need a lecture when everything in that look said, 'My sister gets hurt, I'll kill you'.

Caleb didn't intend to apologise for something that wasn't any of his damn business. "Whatever this is, it has nothing to do with Mia."

"This fucker obviously has anger management issues, whoever he is." Rory jammed his whole fist into one of the new wall decorations. "How do you know he won't come after you next? Or someone close to you?"

Caleb could look after himself, he'd spent a lifetime doing so, but could he stop Mia getting involved? He doubted it. What chance did he have of protecting her when he didn't even know who, or what, he was dealing with himself?

"You think you can stop him? I gotta say, I'm not convinced." Caleb wouldn't roll over and let Rory take charge without a valid reason.

The vibrato of Rory's low growl made Caleb's hackles rise "This bastard shat all over my backyard and scared my little sister. I will hunt him down if it's the last thing I do."

Perhaps having back-up, as livid as he was, might give Caleb the edge over his unknown adversary. With an armed police officer, and one seriously pissed off home owner, this fucker wouldn't know what had hit him when they caught up with him. In the meantime, Mia's safety took precedence over their score settling. Now that Rory had put the thought of her in danger into his head, Caleb was keen to get back and check up on her.

On their return they found Mia and Naomi curled up on the settee watching trashy reality television. The women hastily scooted along to make room for them.

"I hope you don't mind, Rory, but Emily's sleeping in your bedroom." Naomi made cute doe eyes at the big dolt who still hadn't broken out of his funk. To see him this riled over someone he'd yet to cross paths with, Caleb knew he was fucked if he ever messed his sister about.

"Sure." He totally dismissed the single mum with a gruffness that should have been directed elsewhere. Much like Caleb's own behaviour earlier, he suspected.

Now he saw Mia's point about attacking her brother without just cause. It made him question how much of his father's bad qualities he'd inherited along with the house. He knew only too well that a Jackson temper needed taming and he resolved to work on it. After all, he didn't want that part of his father's legacy putting a downer on anyone else's life, when he was still trying to repair the damage to his own.

Mia couldn't help but wonder if they'd undergone some sort of body-swapping experiment while they had been away. Rory took to stomping around the house in the traditional brooding male fashion, whilst Caleb moved back into the spare bedroom without a murmur of dissent.

She looked at Naomi and they both shrugged together. "Men!" Their fit of giggles probably wouldn't have gone down well with either man of the household.

Mia gave Caleb time to get settled in the room before she went in search of him. The faint sound of a guitar drifted across the hall and drew her in like an unfortunate sailor lured by siren song. She found him perched on the end of his bed strumming on one of Rory's old guitars without a care in the world.

"I didn't know you played."

"A little." He practically threw the guitar on the bed when he discovered she was listening. His grin was surprisingly coy for a man who gave the impression that he didn't give a shit about what people thought.

"Do you sing too?" Just when she'd thought she couldn't fancy him any more than she did, he had pulled the ultimate heart throb trump card.

"I used to, in bars for some pin money."

She could imagine him sitting in the corner of a dingy bar, holding the audience captive with some bluesy ballad, and wished she could witness it.

"Maybe you could ask Naomi about getting a gig at The Dog?" It gave her chills to think of him baring his soul. The only thing sexier than having her lover serenade her at work would be if he did it naked.

"I don't know." He carefully placed the guitar back in the corner of the room with Rory's stuff and closed the subject.

Mia didn't push it for now, but, in her mind, this newly discovered talent could provide an income if he chose to stick around. "So, what's going on with you and Rory? I thought you'd rather die of hypothermia than take a room here again."

"Let's say your brother is taking the whole thing very personally. He's making it his mission to track this guy down, and I think he wants me where he can see me." The cryptic reply didn't answer her question fully, but she accepted the change of heart for the sake of harmony. She wouldn't make any more waves if it kept Caleb safe.

"Are you staying the night with me?" A mischievous Caleb abandoned his shyness to slide his hands around her waist.

"I think that might be stretching my brother's hospitality a tad too far, don't you?"

His wicked lips making a necklace of kisses around her throat edged her dangerously close to the point of not caring.

"I can be real quiet." His mouth trailed down to the swell of her cleavage, zapping her every nerve ending with the tip of his tongue.

"I don't think I can." Even with this fully clothed contact she struggled to muffle her moans.

"Oh well. No point getting all riled up for nothing, then, is there?" He backed away, taking his marauding lips with him and immediately cooling her fevered skin.

"Bastard!"

A sharp rap on the door prevented her from throwing him on the bed and having her wicked way regardless.

"Mia? You want a lift home?"

She opened the door to Rory, throwing it wide in a 'see, we aren't doing anything we shouldn't' move. "Sure."

Not only didn't she trust herself to keep her hands off Caleb much longer, but she could take a hint from her grouchy older brother. "Are you taking Naomi and Emily too?"

"No. Er, Naomi's staying overnight." Rory couldn't quite meet her eyes and she couldn't resist teasing him over his obvious crush.

"Oh? Things must be moving very quickly between you two."

A click of his tongue and the clenched jaw expressed his disapproval at the accusation. "Emily is still asleep. It makes more sense for the two of them to stay here. I'll be on the sofa, of course."

"Of course." Her exaggerated smile made him turn on his heels and walk away.

"I'd better go before he leaves me stranded here." The sound of the front door slamming was followed by the car revving in the driveway.

"Yeah, cause it would be tragic if you were stuck here all night. With me." Caleb lifted up the hem of his shirt, revealing inch after inch of taut, tanned skin. That mouthwatering dip of his hip bones into the waistband of his jeans was oh so tempting.

The car horn blared outside to break her from the trance of Caleb's hypnotic abs. He grinned, his ego obviously expanding as rapidly as his dick at her open appreciation.

Frustration bubbled over. She wanted him so badly it hurt, and he knew it. "You're an arsehole!"

"Ah, but you love me for it," Caleb called after her as she walked away.

Yes, I do.

Mia walked to the car in a daze. *Shit!* Falling for him had never been part of the plan, but the son of a bitch with his big brown eyes and unfailing ability to make her smile had made sure of it. All she could do now was pray that he wouldn't break her heart.

Caleb could only take so much of the tiptoeing around Rory's house, trying not to disrupt his routine, or intrude into the possible romance with Naomi. He hid out in his temporary bedroom, but, although he had nothing against the cheery yellow and white décor, his need to break out was all-consuming.

So as not to draw attention, he left via the back door and sprinted into the black woods. He stashed his clothes at the foot of a tree, and, with his human trappings peeled off, gave himself over to his wolf.

Unleashed, he burst through the forest, breathing in the fresh woodland smells he'd recently swapped for paint fumes and domesticity. Onwards he ran, pushing himself to the limit as his breath came in white puffs and his lolling tongue became as dry as sandpaper.

In the distance, his wolf hearing could pick out the trickle of water, and he maintained his breakneck speed until he found the source. A stream gushed down the hillside over rocks and boulders, pooling in ledges perfect for him to drink from.

He lapped the puddles greedily, watching his reflection ripple beneath. A lone wolf stared back, dependent on no one, tied to nothing, yet always thinking about his white wolf mate. How could he mope effectively with her smile permanently stored in his memory for an instant pick-me-up?

When he lifted his head from the pool, he spotted a black wolf looking down on him from the top of the hill. Caleb curled his lip and snarled until the intruder backed out of sight.

It could have been anyone in the community with the same urge as he for a night run, but he spotted it again when he circled the land around his cottage. The coward never came close, always watching from a distance. The skittish creature would scarper every time Caleb snarled or lunged in his direction, but it always came back. Hide and seek never did appeal to Caleb, and he wouldn't waste his time now chasing some young pup with a death wish.

The closer he got to Mia's house, the stronger her scent became. He sniffed the air and howled. The beast in him wouldn't rest without its mate. Apart from the light on the porch, the Blakes' residence slumbered in darkness. Caleb crept around the perimeter using all his senses to pinpoint Mia's location in the house, although the girlie pink curtains and the cuddly wolf toy adorning one particular window easily gave her away.

Finding her bedroom one floor up, Caleb adopted his human body to climb the trellis running along the side of the wall.

"Fuck!" On second thoughts, he wouldn't recommend naked climbing to anyone who wanted to keep their balls intact. He stretched one foot from the trellis over to the window sill, leaving his cock dangling precariously close to the brickwork. Gripping the edge of the window frame, he bridged the gap in one leap. Man, that Romeo guy had taken the easy route to get his girl's attention.

A light went on in the room at the sound of his soft knock. He prayed it wasn't Mrs Blake about to get an eyeful. Mia peeked around the curtain before flinging it wide to take in the spectacle.

"Caleb? What the fuck are you doing?" She opened the window and helped him inside. The frown on her face didn't distract his carnal thoughts from her choice of bed wear.

"I figured fleecy jammies for sure, but, I have to say, I'm far from disappointed." He ducked his head to try to peer underneath the butt-skimming, dusky pink silk.

"Really? You're criticising my outfit?" She arched an eyebrow and swept her gaze over his birthday suit.

"Oh, I'm definitely not criticising, baby." Caleb lifted one of the spaghetti straps with his finger to let it slide off her shoulder and expose one creamy breast. The other strap went next, so the nightie hit the floor and gave him two sweet candies to choose from. The mere sight of her pushed all the events of the day to the back of his mind. Who cared about stray wolves or bricks and mortar when he had this goddess to revere?

He suckled one straining pink tip and rolled the other between his fingers.

"You didn't answer my question." Mia feigned indifference to his oral ministrations, but her body told the truth, arching farther into him.

"I fancied a midnight snack." He nudged her off balance so that she fell onto the bed with a shriek.

"Shh! Your parents will hear us." With that warning, Caleb crawled in between her parted legs.

"They're at the other end of the house." Mia dropped the outrage at his appearance to encourage him.

"Good. We wouldn't want anything spoiling my appetite."

Chapter Seven

Caleb disappeared between her thighs and rescued her from another night of frustration in an empty bed. He lapped at her slit and plunged his tongue into her folds. She pulled at the sheets on the bed, clawing to keep control of her own body. But every orbit of her clit made her submit to his oral skills. He raked his fingernails along her inner thighs, whilst sucking the nub of flesh guaranteed to flood her channel with a river of arousal. He drank every drop.

As if one erogenous zone wasn't enough for him to monopolise, his wayward hand came calling to pinch her nipple and shoot another sharp pain of pleasure straight to her pussy. Like the moon's influence on the oceans' tides, Caleb's every move dictated the ebb and flow of her building climax. Muscle spasms racked her body inside and out, as he pushed her ever closer to climax. When it finally claimed her, those same muscles relaxed as satisfaction spilled over her, and him.

Caleb re-emerged smiling and sporting a hard-on of epic proportions. "I really wanted to come with you then."

"Who's stopping you?" Now that she'd enjoyed herself almost until unconsciousness, she saw no reason he couldn't do the same.

Mia gripped his face in her hands and pulled him up eye level with her. "Your turn."

A shimmy down the bed and she took his staff in her hand, wrapping her lips around the engorged head. Caleb's gasp and the tremble rippling through his body spurred her on to take him deeper into her throat.

She pumped him as she sucked, working her fingers and mouth in tandem to bring the first taste of his salty essence to her tongue. Caleb grabbed at her breasts with a desperation she knew would leave her with bruises. She slipped his cock from between her lips and lodged him between her cleavage.

With as much gusto as if he was inside her, Caleb thrust and Mia rewarded him with a flick of her tongue over the crown of his penis.

"Fuck! Mia!"

Enclosed in the fleshy valley of her breasts, he finally lost his cool. Mia watched as base need governed his actions, securing his hold on her bosom to stay tightly sheathed within. The unforgiving grip and friction against her delicate skin were worth it to see that expression of unadulterated lust painted on his face. With one last groan, he took himself in hand and shot hot cum to jewel her neck.

When his orgasm subsided and they clung together in the sticky aftermath, Caleb peered at the mess frosting her skin. "Now what?"

"Now, we shower. Well, there are some perks to having rich parents." A personal bathroom was one of them.

She led him to the cubicle and turned on the water. Once inside, Caleb took the shower head and waved it across her breasts, washing away all evidence of his climax. Mia copied the action, watching the water sluice over his cut-glass pecs.

A squirt of strawberries and cream shower gel coated her breasts in more goo, which Caleb dutifully rubbed in. With the shower head returned to its rightful place, she stood back under the stream of water to wash away the suds. He slicked his hands over her body, paying particular care to her nether regions. Her legs trembled as he dipped his fingers in and out, creating a void that she desperately needed filled.

Caleb's erection stood proud and tall in the wake of his handiwork, but he refused her silent plea to join their bodies together. Instead, he withdrew from her altogether and unhooked the shower head once again. She waited with hitched breath as he turned up the temperature dial.

"Open your legs."

She did as he commanded, regardless that her first instinct was to close them. *He won't hurt you.* The upturned shower head spurted fountains of water between her legs.

"Are you fucking kidding me? I don't want my lady bits steam cleaned thanks."

"Trust me."

She relaxed as much as she could with the hot implement getting closer to her delicate parts. It brushed against her pussy lips, the moreish sensation of the hot water stinging her swollen folds. The heat definitely added a new dimension to her arousal. Suddenly she understood that connection between hot candle wax and sex that appealed to so many in the erotic novels she'd read in secret.

Once upon a time she wouldn't have dared to voice an opinion on what she did or didn't want in the bedroom. Maybe before Caleb had come along she hadn't even known what that had been, but now, with him as her mentor, everything had become clear.

"Caleb, you'd better fuck me right now or I'll kick your arse." She surprised herself by the sexually assertive woman she'd turned into. He'd created a monster.

His chuckle didn't bode well. Neither did the sound of him shutting off the water. "Here's a novel idea. Why don't we actually take this to the bed for a change?"

He took Mia by the hand and led her through to the bedroom. Caleb wanted to show her he had more to offer than a quick bang against a bookcase, or a knee-shattering romp on a hard floor. After their somewhat explosive foreplay earlier, he figured they could take a bit more time and make this more than just getting their rocks off — as pleasant as that had been up until now.

Mia stretched out onto the covers and waited for him, a wet dream in every sense. Yet there was something almost virginal about her beautifully naked body fresh from the shower. Lying on a bed of pink and white flowers, her hair spread upon the pillow in a golden halo like Botticelli's Venus, he was afraid to defile her. Until she spoke.

"Are you going to get your butt over here, or am I going to have to take care of myself?" The mischievous tone of her voice prompted him to join her and follow his lady's request.

In keeping with her playful mood, Caleb pounced onto the bed, growling as he trapped her between his arms. "What's your hurry? We've got all night."

Those big blue eyes looking up, so full of trust, knocked him for six. His resolve wavered momentarily as he dipped his head to kiss her mouth. That simple indulgence was enough to hook him again, so every touch of her skin felt like the first time.

Their lips fitted together in perfect sync, matching each other's need in passionate, relentless pressure. Mia's tongue tangled with his, as he lowered himself onto the bed to take her in his arms. Caleb couldn't get enough of her, sweeping his hands down her slender back to cup her buttocks, while his lips never strayed from hers.

"The condoms are in the drawer," Mia mumbled against his mouth. He reached across to rummage in the bedside cabinet, trying not to break contact with her. Once he'd dressed for the occasion, he slipped inside Mia with ease. Lying side by side, they moved slowly, their unhurried lovemaking a revelation for them both.

Mia held him in place, drawing both legs up around his waist to give him unlimited access to plunder her sex. He kissed her neck as she clung to him, her gasps warming his skin as they rocked together. As she verbalised her increasing excitement, she also strengthened their bond. The sensation of her inner muscles squeezing around his girth sent him scaling those heady heights before he was ready.

He grabbed hold of her, attempting to stem the intensity of their connection, but the feel of her hips thrusting with such wild abandon was too gratifying to tame. They worked in unison, bodies rising and falling as they climbed the crest of ecstasy. Mia bit down on his shoulder when she climaxed, the cream of her orgasm gushing around him. The unexpected primitive act shattered Caleb's restraint and he came so hard and fast that it left him dizzy.

Something changed for him as he poured everything he had into her. This was more than getting sweaty with a gorgeous girl. He needed her. Looking back now, he'd spent his whole life searching for the peace only she brought him. Mia soothed that rage in his soul that he'd thought could never be extinguished. As he held her in his arms, Caleb knew she was the one. His only.

"You have to go." Mia popped his bubble with the prick of reality. "Mum and Dad can't find you here, and Rory will wonder where you are."

"Give me five minutes. You really took it out of me, you know. Who would have thought you were a biter?" He burrowed under the covers with her, unwilling to face the outside world and the judgement that came with it. If it meant he could stay here with her he would take the consequences of outstaying his welcome.

"Excuse me? You were the one who turned up bollock naked and hornier than a horned, horny thing from Horny Town. You should be thanking me for easing your suffering. As for the biting, well, it was better than screaming the house down." She grinned and plucked his nipple to a bullet point. The tweak she gave it restarted his Mia addiction and trampled over any thoughts of sleep.

"In that case, let me thank you properly." He grabbed her hand and rolled her onto her back, silencing her faux protest with a kiss.

Circumstances beyond his control meant that a future together wasn't an option, but while he had her exactly where he wanted her, Caleb was determined to make it last. For however long they had together.

* * * *

Having fallen asleep soon after their last bout of naked wrestling, Caleb barely made it out of the house before Mia's parents rose. His clothes were damp with morning dew when he retrieved them, but he wore them nonetheless in case he should run into Rory.

Maybe that, or his all night exertions, was the cause of his current discomfort. His skin clammy, his stomach rolling, and his limbs aching, he collapsed into bed as darkness captured him.

"Caleb? Caleb?" Some time later, Mia's frantic voice peered under the heavy veil pinning him down. Too tired to let the outside world in, he turned over and sank back into unconsciousness.

He snuggled into the pillow and let pictures of Mia brighten his darkness.

The black wolf lurked in the recess of his mind, waiting to attack. She smiled and laughed, dancing on the porch. The sound of claws tapping on the wooden walkway approached from behind her. The wolf pounced. Mia screamed.

"No!" Caleb sprang up, perspiration soaking his skin.

"Are you okay?" Mia placed her hand on his forehead.

"You're here? You're safe?" It took a moment for his scrambled thoughts to untangle into some semblance of sense.

"I'm fine. It's you I'm worried about." Mia pressed a cold flannel against his burning cheeks.

"Me?" The room started to spin, and, content she was safe, Caleb slumped back onto the bed.

"You're sick."

"It's been said..." He closed his eyes and simply enjoyed her company.

"No. I mean really sick. I think you've come down with whatever Emily has."

Snatches of muted conversations replayed in his head, memories drifting back to haunt him like the morning after a heavy drinking session. "Who was here?"

"Naomi found you when you didn't come down for breakfast. Rory wasn't in a fit state to help either, so she called me. The doctor says it's a virus. It took some persuading on our part that your temperature didn't warrant a hospital stay without revealing the whole 'wolves run hot' deal, I can tell you. But he agreed to let you stay put providing you get lots of rest and drink plenty of fluids." She reached over to the bedside table to pour him a glass of water, which he accepted with shaking hands. All the after-effects of a hangover without a drop of alcohol crossing his lips.

"Rory's sick too?" His foggy brain finally caught up with the whole conversation.

"He's denying it, of course, but his complexion is the same grey-green as yours, and he can barely lift a coffee cup." Mia's depiction of a frail Rory was akin to admitting that Santa Claus doesn't exist. It took away some of the magic in the legend.

"And Emily?" If the illness was capable of rendering both he and the burly policeman into pathetic mortals, he pitied the child a great deal.

"A bit listless, but she's sleeping it off. It looks like you're all quarantined here for the foreseeable future."

"Suits me. I don't mind being holed up with my sexy nurse." He waited for her to squeeze in beside him. They may as well make the most of it, even if Mia would probably have to do most of the work until he regained his energy.

"Uh-uh. You are quarantined, not me, and your disease-ridden body isn't coming near me any time soon." The bed sprung up as she got to her feet.

"Don't go." He grabbed her wrist, wanting her to play nurse for a while longer.

"You need to rest, and I need a cuppa." A swift kiss to his brow gave him some comfort before she departed and left him to drift back into an easy sleep.

"How's the patient?" Naomi set a mug in front of her. With a day spent stressing out over others, they were both powered solely by coffee, and Mia could have done with something stronger.

"Still a bit loopy, but he'll be okay."

When Naomi had phoned to say he'd collapsed, Mia had gone through a panic she never wanted to experience again. The fear for his welfare, for her sanity if he came to any harm, suddenly eclipsed her petty troubles with her parents, although she may have overplayed her role in Rory's convalescence in order to explain her absence to them. Having dropped everything, and everyone, to race to his bedside, it was clear that she was in deeper than she'd ever anticipated.

"How's Em?" She needed to focus on something other than the mess of her emotions.

"I got her to take some liquid paracetamol that seems to be bringing her temperature down at least. She's bundled up on the sofa watching cartoons now, so I think she's coming around." The worry lines on Naomi's face had begun to smooth out.

"It's probably only a twenty-four hour bug. They'll all be grand by tomorrow." Mia didn't know how else to comfort her friend when she didn't go in for PDAs. Words were so much more difficult than a good old hug.

"Poor Rory and Caleb. It's my fault they're sick too. If only I hadn't been so stubborn about taking charge of the delivery and just picked Emily up myself, none of this would have happened." It was typical of her boss to assume responsibility for a situation no one could have seen coming.

"They'll get over it. They're strapping big men, even if they are weak as puppies right now. What I don't understand is how hard this virus has hit them. Shifters aren't usually so prone to these things." She didn't enjoy seeing her brother and lover so vulnerable, one little bit. Given a choice, she'd much rather have the overbearing, smart-arses back to full strength.

"Maybe it's a rare strain that they, we, haven't encountered before." Naomi downed the coffee, still too hot for Mia's palate, and left the conversation to rinse her cup.

"Is Caleb awake yet?" Rory staggered into the kitchen, wearing nothing but his boxers and holding onto the walls for support.

"I've spoken to him and he's under the same orders as you. Get back to bed!" Mia shooed him back towards the bedroom, ducking under one beefy arm to prop him up.

"I have things to do." He slumped against her. *Please God don't fall on me!*

"Rory, you can barely walk. I don't think you'll be much use to anyone for the next couple of days." This role reversal made her appreciate how much effort it took to look after a sibling, and he'd been doing it his entire life. Perhaps she *was* the millstone in their relationship, and not the other way around. He'd put his life on hold to chaperone her through hers.

"Maybe I'll go back to bed for an hour and see how I feel." His bare feet trailed on the carpet and Mia struggled with the heavy load.

"Good idea, Einstein." The sarcasm was lost on her zoned-out brother, but it made her feel better to keep things normal.

Naomi came to her rescue and took some of the burden on her shoulders. Between them they manoeuvred his bulk into his room, vacated by the previous patient, and laid him on the bed.

"Thanks, hon." Eyes already closed, he mumbled, and his soft snores followed them out of the door.

Their laughter masked their concern for all involved in the outbreak.

"What will we do about work?" They couldn't both stay here and let Naomi neglect her business indefinitely.

She peered around the door to check on Emily and closed it quietly behind her. "I don't want to leave her until I can see an improvement. Could you open up for me, Mia?"

"Sure." It was a huge step for Naomi to ask for her help. Mia plastered on a smile, and, with all her instructions memorised, she set off to the pub. Even though her heart remained by Caleb's bedside.

* * * *

The day dragged slower than a tortoise on muscle relaxants. Any notion that work would take her mind off the patients evaporated with the constant questions and best wishes from the patrons. Naomi and Rory's simultaneous disappearance had caused quite a stir.

"Have the young lovers done a moonlit flit?"

"No such scandal, I'm afraid. Emily and Rory are down with a virus. Caleb too. Naomi's looking after them all," she repeated for the hundredth time, counting down the minutes until someone relieved her of her duties, so she could join them.

Although she wanted an hourly update on their condition, she refrained from telephoning in case she woke anyone. She didn't even have her mobile to text, since she'd left the house in such a flap that morning. The minute hand on the clock above the bar dragged slowly. When the phone rang out the back, Mia sprinted to answer it.

"Hello?"

"How are things?" Naomi's voice on the other end improved her mood no end.

"Ticking along. How are the patients?" Impatience fizzed in her veins waiting for news.

"Caleb and Rory are still asleep, but Emily's wide awake. She's managed to eat a piece of toast and drink some milk, so I think she's on the mend."

"Thank goodness." Mia wanted to reach down the phone and give her a great big hug whether she wanted it or not.

"Since Emily's on her feet, maybe we should do a swap for a while?" Naomi echoed her own thoughts.

"Certainly. We can take it turnabout between the bar and the sick house." Keeping all bases covered. "And before you ask, yes, I'll call you every fifteen minutes with an Emily progress check."

Like a greyhound out of a race trap, Mia bolted as soon as Naomi appeared at The Dog. It eased her conscience, along with her worry levels, to be close to Caleb and Rory, even if she could do nothing to improve their condition.

* * * *

Rory struggled back to bed when she arrived to take over his child-minding duties. As reported, Emily now toddled about quite happily, though her cheeks remained on the rosy side.

"What are we going to do with you, missy?" Mia swung the child up into her arms and was presented with a half-chewed picture book. "Ah, I see. Story time."

After regaling her with tales of woodland animals, complete with character voices, Mia tucked Emily under the duvet on the sofa. Her giggles and hugs had been a welcome sign of her continued recovery, a relief to Mia on behalf of her friend and as a forecast for Caleb and Rory's condition.

Once Emily was settled, she went to check on the boys' progress. Rory was flaked out on top of his bed, although he did look more human than reptilian today. On opening the door to Caleb's room she was shocked to find the rumpled covers missing her sick puppy.

"You looking for me?" The sound of him alone raised the hairs on the back of her neck.

"Yeah. If you're feeling better then perhaps I should go home." Regardless that his breath smelt all minty fresh, and the scent of soap lingered on his skin, it wasn't the time or the place for her to start getting all het up again.

"Stay." The simple request provided reason enough for her to continue her vigil, but the slight buckling of his knees as he entered the room sealed the deal.

"All right, but only if you get back into bed until you are one hundred per cent better." It was easier to resist him when he still resembled a foal trying to get used to his legs.

"Yes, ma'am." His obedience confirmed there was a way to go in his recovery, when he was too tired to try anything on with her, but obviously even just showering had taken an effort. She appreciated the sentiment and looked forward to making up for lost time.

Mia dodged an attempt to kiss her as she plumped his pillows and fixed the sheets around him. "We can't afford for any more of us to get sick. Naomi and I are both run ragged between here, The Dog, and nipping home for stuff we need."

"I know. I appreciate it. You know, I could get used to having someone looking after me."

"The sooner you're back on your feet, the better for us all." Being so intimate with him when he was naked and vulnerable had her tied in knots. Each time she fed or bathed him, he stole another piece of her heart. Every day she spent with him was a step closer to a broken heart.

Chapter Eight

"I'm surprised you don't just move in." Forty-eight hours later, Rory wandered into the kitchen, past where Mia sat at his table, and went straight to the fridge.

"What makes you say that?" She screwed up her nose as he gulped orange juice from the carton. He had a point. The phone calls from her mother checking in on her every five minutes were getting beyond a joke.

"You know as well as I do Caleb's fine. You two are milking it so you can spend more time together." He wiped his mouth and helped himself to a slice of the toast she'd buttered for Caleb.

Too stunned to move, she let him snaffle a second piece. "Wh-what?"

"Mia, I've known from the minute you clapped eyes on each other you were both smitten. I don't know what all the secrecy is in aid of." He added a banana to his breakfast on the go, with his appetite apparently fully restored.

With no forthcoming lecture or judgement coming from her brother, she didn't bother to deny it. "It's nothing serious. You heard him, he's selling up and moving on, remember." Saying it aloud actually physically hurt. She doubled over as pains shot through her abdomen.

"If that happens, I'll strip naked and dance through the pub." He reached for the last piece of toast.

This time she did slap his hand away. "Eww! I hope you're right. For the sake of public decency, if nothing else."

"Honestly, Mia. Anyone with eyes can see how he feels about you."

"And you're okay with that?" Rory's reaction was part of the reason they'd kept this secret. She'd expected if he'd found out to be locked away in a tower somewhere, guarded by slavering beasts, with Caleb's body parts dispatched to the four corners of the earth.

Rory fixed her with his serious older brother stare. "It has fuck all to do with me, Mia. But, for the record, I think Caleb's a decent guy."

This blessing of sorts showed how much she'd misjudged her brother's attitude towards her. All this time she'd thought his presence too stifling in her life. She could see now that it had been nothing more than him looking out for his little sis while their parents had concentrated on their careers and social standing.

"What about Mum and Dad? They'll go mental if they find out about Caleb, when they're still pushing Robbie at me." Their lofty dreams for a wealthy son-in-law, with Mia as a kept woman, were a far cry from her ideal. All she wanted was her independence to work where she wanted, and be with a man she loved. Caleb.

"For fuck's sake, Mia! You're a grown woman, and as soon as you start acting that way, and making decisions for yourself, the sooner they'll treat you like one. Mum will keep trying to run your life for as long as you let her. I thought, when you packed in your studies and dumped Robbie, you were finally standing up for yourself. But you've fallen back into that baby of the family role, where we all think we have to take care of you. As for Caleb, I'd vouch for him over that pussy Robbie any day of the week." The brutally honest outburst, so uncharacteristic of her stoic brother, left her open-mouthed and struggling for words to retaliate. Rory's home truths stung more than she cared to admit. As always, he was annoyingly accurate in his assessment.

"I'm not sure it's even worth the hassle of telling them about Caleb." Why face her mother's screaming ab-dabs over something that wouldn't last?

"Morning." Caleb strode in, his jeans slung low around his hips, and showing off a chest that wouldn't have looked out of place in a sexy aftershave ad.

When he went straight to the kettle instead of to her, Mia worried he'd heard her conversation with Rory

"Good to see you up and about, mate." Rory sensibly changed the subject, but Caleb's appearance had opened her eyes to her mistake. He was totally worth it.

"Yeah, well, I think it's time I stopped feeling sorry for myself and got back to work." Caleb dropped a kiss on her head as he passed, easing her fears.

"Work?" Mia's spirits lifted. Actively seeking work surely meant he would stay.

"The cottage isn't going to sell itself. Is it?" Caleb cruelly dashed her hopes and dreams to the ground, with a smile she couldn't imitate.

"Do you want me to help out? Emily's back at nursery now, so I have a few hours to spare." Since Naomi and Emily's departure, and Mia's child-minding services becoming surplus to requirement, she had found herself missing the little girl.

She didn't think of herself as particularly maternal, nor did she ever get broody. The rapport she'd developed with Emily had come as a pleasant surprise. Perhaps she should look into childcare as an actual career, instead of pulling pints and wiping tables.

"No. You need a break after the hours you've put in here. Besides, the last time I was there I saw a black wolf prowling around. Smaller than Rory, before you ask, and wiry. He was too far away for me to track his scent." Caleb's latest news brought a frown to her brother's brow, and no wonder. They both knew this other wolf well.

"Robbie?"

"Sounds like it." Rory confirmed her suspicions.

"But why?"

"Jealousy? If he knows we're together it would give him motive, for sure. A spineless arsehole like that wouldn't think twice about something as underhand as trashing an empty house." Caleb's impression of her ex was pretty much on the money. Whilst he hadn't exactly swept her off her feet with passion and romance, Robbie wouldn't take too kindly to her moving on either.

"There's one problem with that theory. The first attack happened before you got here, Caleb. Unless he's psychic, Robbie couldn't have known about you two." Rory threw the facts at them, but Mia couldn't completely dismiss the idea of Robbie's involvement.

She knew first-hand how ruthless he could be in his pursuits.

They had been thrown together at a young age, with their parents attending the same golf club lunches and charity functions. She should have listened to her instincts telling her he was weak and devious as the years went on. Of course, the joint secret of their families' heritage had meant that they had gravitated towards each other at these events, but even when she'd turned down his advances, he'd pursued her via her parents. The flowers, the presents and the coincidental meetings virtually every time they left the house had made him impossible to ignore. Looking back now, the stalkery tendencies had been there to see, but the continual coaxing from her mother had brainwashed her into thinking they should be a couple.

He'd always treated her like a possession—something to flaunt in front of others, and discard when he was bored. The spoilt child in him had probably seen what she had with Caleb and wanted it for himself. Rory was right, though, that didn't explain the timing of the attacks.

"Maybe I should renew my acquaintance with Master Carson and see what he's up to?" The thought alone turned her stomach. She didn't want to even be in the same room as him, but she would do whatever it took to put an end to Caleb's torment.

"You do whatever you think is necessary, babe." Caleb left her to her own devices as he went to get dressed. The casual attitude to her suggestion pissed her off. *I'm putting myself on the line here!* Mia worried their time was already coming to an end when he didn't make a big deal about keeping her safe from harm.

Limbs too tired to make the transition to wolf, Caleb settled for his neglected Thunderbird to break free from his emotional confines. Through his fevered haze, he'd envisaged a life here. A home with someone who loved him had seemed within his grasp. All those hopes had vanished with Mia's cutting words. He simply wasn't worth the hassle.

Worthless. Stupid. His father's words resurfaced to torment him.

He sped up, trying to outrun his inadequacies. Now what? Did he go along with the pretence that she wanted him here and take advantage of Rory's charity? Or man up, accept the inevitable and head for the hills? He could keep going, follow this road to wherever and start again. He was good at that.

The road curved and he leaned into the bend. A black shape darted in front of his wheels. He swerved, but his precarious position toppled him over and sent the bike skidding.

Lying winded in the middle of the road, he saw the dark figure weaving through the undergrowth. The black wolf. When it saw he was incapacitated, it came to circle his body, sniffing and snarling. So brave now. Through the visor of his helmet, Caleb could make out the look of superiority in the wolf's eyes that could only be Robbie.

With arrogant grace, the wolf stepped over him to where the motorbike lay immobile. It lifted its leg and pissed over Caleb's pride and joy. If a wolf could smirk, Caleb was sure he had witnessed it before the beast crept back into the long grass

Despite feeling like road kill, Caleb managed to remove his helmet and take deep, heaving breaths. Only the notion that he could end up under someone else's wheels gave him enough impetus to get back on his feet. The torn patches of skin and bruised ribs would heal quickly, but for now they hurt like fuck.

He hobbled over to the bike and heaved it upright. The screaming pain in his chest and the jellied condition of his legs made it impossible for him to get back on. Using it as a crutch instead, he headed back to the cottage. Now he knew what he had to do.

* * * *

"Oh my God. Caleb! What the hell happened to you?" Mia rushed across the bar to check him over so thoroughly that he could almost believe she cared.

"I came off the bike." The cuts and bruises must have looked as bad as they felt, judging by her horrified reaction.

"Are you okay?"

He shrugged off the small hands touching his face, suddenly irritated by the open display of affection.

"I'm fine. It's no big deal, it happens all the time." *Usually without the assistance of someone's murderous ex-boyfriend.*

"No big deal? Look at the state of you." She gestured at the raw skin showing through his ripped clothes.

"Don't worry. It won't happen again." He carried on over to the bar and ordered a beer from a shell-shocked Naomi.

"What do you mean? You can't know that for sure." Mia really didn't have the right to play the nagging other half when she clearly only wanted him for one thing.

He took a sip of beer. "I sold my bike."

"You did what?"

If only he'd kept his fridge stocked at home, he wouldn't have had to endure her fake concern.

"I don't need it for now, but I do need the cash to pay for the house repairs." The dealer had been only too glad to get his hands on the bike. Caleb could always get a new one with the proceeds from the house sale.

"But you love that bike."

"Love isn't all it's cracked up to be. Is it?" Another mouthful of beer dulled the hurt he was desperately trying to manage, then he walked away to the gents' before she could badger him for any more information.

He faced his mangled reflection in the mirror and dabbed wet tissue paper on the scrapes and scratches. Selling his T-Bird was the way forward, the only financial means of getting out of this nightmare. In the meantime he predicted his wolf would get a lot of exercise, running off his nervous energy when he'd healed. Once he'd tidied himself as much as possible, he went back to the bar and his only ally—beer.

On his return, he found Robbie draped over the counter. Caleb's first instinct was to slam the fucker's head repeatedly into the wood, but he settled for a beer beside the fireplace instead. The heat took the chill from his weary body, but even the smell of logs burning in the hearth couldn't mask Robbie's now familiar scent. That sickly sweet perfume of self-importance and wealth assaulted Caleb's senses. The black wolf had marked the territory around the cottage and left no doubt in his mind that Robbie was responsible for the damage. If only he could figure out why.

Mia fought back the tears Caleb's cold demeanour had called to the fore. After a week of looking after him, getting so close, she could sense him now backing away. Creating that distance between them so he found it easier to leave.

Only Robbie's arrival had halted her outpouring of misery. She wouldn't give him the satisfaction of seeing her upset. "What can I get you?"

"I'll have a whisky, and whatever you're having." He held a twenty-pound note between his fingers, and she snatched it away without touching him.

"No thanks. I'm working." Her skin crawled to think she'd ever been with this man. He couldn't hold a candle to Caleb.

"What about after work?" His hand deliberately brushed hers as he took his change.

Mia's gaze inadvertently travelled over to Caleb brooding in the corner, willing him to come rescue her.

"Are you two together then?" Robbie swirled the liquid around his glass, not bothering to turn around.

Her pulse skittered and her stomach knotted. She wouldn't tell him even if she'd known the answer for sure. "He's leaving as soon as the cottage is sold."

"You need someone who can provide for you, who can give you the life you deserve." He took a delicate sip of the whisky. Behind him, Caleb knocked back his beer with that masculine swagger that set them so far apart.

"And that's you, is it?" Caleb came 'sold as seen', whereas Robbie was more of a showpiece, his fancy exterior hiding all manner of cracks and flaws.

"It could be." He set his glass down and tried to make another grab for her hand. She pulled it away in time.

"No. It couldn't. You can't bully me into loving you, Robbie. You tried that once before, remember?" The constant phone calls and messages had nearly driven her to the brink of madness, until she'd finally agreed to let him play some small part in her life again. Instead of severing all contact first time around, that mistake had led him, and her mother, to believe they still had a chance.

As usual, what she wanted didn't enter into Robbie's scheme of things. "You know I bought the Henstridge Farm?" He primped his imaginary feathers and puffed out his chest.

"Yes." She didn't care. This peacocking never did impress her, but Robbie always insisted on playing the big man. She let him prattle on while she carried on serving around him.

"I'm thinking of putting an offer in on the Jackson place too, with it being the adjoining property." Robbie's words finally made an impact on her.

"You can't buy Caleb's house!" The ground rushed up to meet her and she clung to the bar top to stop her falling. She couldn't imagine anyone living there except Caleb, didn't want anyone else there. It was too soon.

Robbie's haughty laugh rubbed more salt in the wound. "Why on earth not? He wants to sell. I want to buy. I could end up a big player around here if I secure both properties."

His shark-like determination gave Mia the chills. With hindsight, it was entirely possible that his dogged pursuit of her had probably had more to do with her family's sizeable estate, rather than her winning personality.

"Good luck to you." That was all she could manage before she had to go and throw up.

* * * *

Caleb's disappearing act from the pub meant that she had to wait until after work to pass on the information she'd gleaned from Robbie. Finally tracking him down to Rory's, she was able to tell them both about the new development at the same time.

"Robbie's after your land. He's the one who bought the Henstridge place and he thinks if he gets yours too it'll make him some sort of property mogul." She waited for Caleb's reaction, expecting him to come out swinging for her ex. Nothing. The passion he'd once displayed so willingly now seemed to have fizzled out.

It was Rory who got animated, pacing and gesticulating as he spoke. "That certainly gives the bastard motive. Let me chase a few things up."

He left the room, mobile already fastened to his ear with a look of determination that Caleb didn't share. No, the victim of Robbie's campaign remained in his seat, emotionless, staring out of the window like she wasn't even there.

Well, she cared enough for both of them. The love in her heart for him was greater than her parents' disdain, or Robbie's tyranny. Somehow she had to find a way to make Caleb stay. Easier said than done with the void between them creating such an awkward atmosphere. She wanted to ask what had changed, or curl up in his lap and kiss him until the sun went down. But either of those actions could send him running in the other direction.

Until he gave her an opening to discuss her feelings, she wouldn't add to his problems. Not once did he express a wish to put down roots here, so she couldn't expect to live happily ever after with him.

Rory eventually returned to break the uncomfortable silence. "The estate agent confirmed Robbie made that first laughable offer."

"I don't understand where he's getting the money to fund this venture. Unless he has some secret fortune stashed away somewhere." Although he lived a lavish lifestyle, Mia knew Mummy and Daddy provided most of that for him.

"Someone like Robbie will have connections. I'm sure he's a bank manager's wet dream. Boy Wonder will have secured loans no problem." Rory leant forward in his seat, more animated about proceedings than Caleb, who sat examining the scabs forming on his elbows.

"Caleb? Thoughts?" Desperate to see him fight for his property, for her, she very nearly gave him a slap upside the head.

He shrugged.

Her palm itched.

"We know Robbie trashed the place, probably to lower the price or scare me off. We can't prove it, though. Even if we could, his is the only offer I have on the books."

Mia's blood ran cold. "You're not seriously thinking of selling to him after everything?"

Rory moved over to Caleb's chair, and for a split second she thought he might grab Caleb and give him the shake he deserved. "Don't let the scumbag get away with it, Caleb. You're worth ten of him."

Caleb narrowed his eyes. "Really? I thought I wasn't worth the hassle?"

Horror filled her belly as he repeated her words. Rory tactfully left the room to let them speak in private.

"I didn't mean it like that—"

"No. You're right. It's not worth getting into an argument with your parents over me when I'm nothing more to you than a leg-over."

How she regretted those words—especially now as he stood before her, his wounds raw, and entirely her fault.

"I'm scared of loving you, Caleb. That's the only reason I said it. I didn't want to admit how I felt about you when you're so dead set about leaving." A sob ripped from her throat as her heart cracked wide open.

Caleb walked over to her, bridging that gap, and held her by the shoulders. "Forget everything else—Rory, your parents, Robbie, what might or might not happen—and look inside your heart. Figure out exactly how you feel about me and what it is you want."

"I love you. I want only you." She didn't need time to figure it out. For all her indecisiveness and fears, of this she was certain.

The crushing weight of his silence bore down on her until her poor heart threatened to give up the ghost. Luckily, Caleb moved into action with some mouth to mouth to revive her.

"Does this mean you'll stay?" As much as she needed this kiss, she also wanted to hear him say it.

"Yes. For as long as you want me here, I'll stay. We might have to take care of our little rodent problem before we get to spend cosy nights in, but I'm willing to give us a go." As romantic declarations went, it ranked somewhere alongside 'get your coat, you've pulled', but Mia would take it.

At least he was giving them a chance to be together, and if Robbie was the biggest obstacle on her path to happiness, she would take every step within her power to physically remove him.

Chapter Nine

"Remind me why I'm doing this." Caleb sat slumped in the passenger seat, a cloud of impending doom settling over the car as they pulled up to the house.

"Because you love my sister, and you owe it to her to make this work." Rory's voice of reason only served to darken Caleb's mood.

He didn't want to be reasonable. He wanted to be headstrong and stubborn and run away before he faced the strength of his feelings for Mia. By agreeing to stay and invest in a future here with her, he was opening himself up for all kinds of hurt. No one had ever got that close to him. He didn't know how to be what she wanted, needed, and it scared the shit out of him.

The car stopped and Rory got out, beckoning him to get a move on. Like a death row inmate walking the mile, he took his time, relishing his last moments before he faced his execution.

"Caleb." Mr Blake nodded a welcome at the front door. At least he wasn't brandishing a shotgun after the last eventful visit.

"Mr Blake. Mrs Blake." He returned the civil greeting, although Mia's mother clutched her husband close as if she expected some sort of attack.

Caleb took a deep breath, and the first step to reconciliation. "Can I just apologise for my behaviour here during the dinner. I was rude and obnoxious. I'm sorry if I ruined your evening."

Gayle smiled a little too brightly, but accepted the olive branch. "Not at all, Caleb. I understand it was a difficult time, so soon after your father's death."

"Thank you." While he didn't agree with her assessment, he acknowledged the sentiment in hope that it would make tonight flow smoother.

To walk in on Robbie then, cosied up beside Mia in the lounge, nearly knocked him on his arse. Mia ditched the sleaze and rushed over to meet Caleb and Rory, grabbing two beers on the way.

"Thanks for coming." She kissed Caleb on the cheek. He enjoyed both her touch and Robbie's seething reaction.

Caleb splayed his hand around her waist in a possessive hold designed to wind him up even further. Mia ignored the one-upmanship and took him to meet the other guests at her impromptu drinks soirée.

"This is Mr and Mrs Carson. Robbie's parents." The well-groomed couple bore the same dark hair and pinched features as their son.

"Pleased to meet you." He shook hands and exchanged pleasantries like any other civilised member of society, without revealing a glimmer of the intense hatred he bore for their offspring.

"I hear you're selling the house." Mr Carson got straight down to business while his wife exuded boredom beside him.

"Not any longer. I've decided to stay put." Caleb made sure he'd said it loud enough for everyone to hear, especially Robbie. It worked.

"You can't!" The snivelling little shit jumped in to interrupt their conversation.

Caleb watched the colour drain from his face with great satisfaction. "Why not, Robbie?"

"You said you were leaving. I want the cottage." Caleb half expected Robbie to stomp his foot and demand that Daddy buy him anything he wanted.

Mia slipped her hand into Caleb's. "You heard him, Robbie. He's staying. And I'm moving in with him." That surprised everyone in the room, Caleb included.

"You are?" The thought distracted Caleb from their game of 'Get Robbie to Spill his Guts'. Yes, he found the prospect of making love to her every evening and waking up to her each morning very appealing.

"I am." Her assertive response didn't quite match the worry still showing in her eyes. Caleb squeezed her hand to show that he wholeheartedly supported the idea.

"You can still sell me the cottage and move somewhere else." Robbie ran a finger around the collar of his buttoned-up shirt.

"Um, we don't want to, Robbie." Caleb gave him the same smirk Robbie had used with him once too often.

"Robbie. What on earth has gotten into you? You're making a show of yourself," Daddy dearest scolded his son but Robbie continued to splutter and sweat.

"I only bought the Henstridge place because I thought he would sell that piece of shit too."

"I'm quite happy with that 'piece of shit'. If only I could stop the sneaky bastard who keeps trashing it in the hope I'll sell it for half of what it's worth." Caleb made the most of having the upper hand in the room, as both the Carsons and the Blakes gasped.

"I need that fucking land!" Robbie's pale features bulged and flushed scarlet, until Caleb thought he might explode on the good Axminster. Revenge tasted sweet on Caleb's tongue.

Mr Carson tried to bundle Robbie out of the room but he was too far gone to know when to stop. "I can't develop a golf course on one poxy plot of land, you fucking moron. What do you need it for, except to use as a dog toilet?" Wrestling free from his father's grasp, his hair mussed and clothes askew, he appeared even more deranged than his actions had suggested.

"What are you talking about? What golf course?" Mr Carson asked the question most prevalent in Caleb's mind.

Robbie rolled his eyes. "We have some of the best land there is here in Olcan Hills. It's wasted on scruffy mutts like him."

"What golf course?" Mia's father now demanded the answer.

"I'm in talks with an American investor to develop the land in a deal worth millions. A little scrote like Jackson here isn't going to get in my way." Robbie's threats didn't scare Caleb. Not now that he'd exposed his plans to all and sundry.

"You can't build a golf course here," Gayle Blake chimed in, apparently more horrified by Robbie's dastardly deals than the idea of Mia moving into the cottage.

"It would ruin the community." With female solidarity, Mrs Carson joined in the condemnation of her son.

"It's not happening, son. I don't care how much it's worth. We won't destroy our community by shipping in a load of tourists simply to line your pocket." Mr Carson was right. They couldn't hope to survive if they were exposed as wolf shifters to the world.

The one outstanding feature of this area was the privacy afforded the occupants to live as both wolf and human. An influx of new blood would destroy their civilisation.

"But, Dad, I've already bought the Henstridge place," Robbie whined but he'd lost any power he'd once held.

"I bought the Henstridge place as an investment. Unless you want to end up in jail for the damage you've almost certainly caused to Mr Jackson's property, you will sign it back to me." His father took the last word on the subject as Robbie hung his head in defeat.

* * * *

Mia sat in stunned silence with Caleb and the rest of the family for a long time after the Carsons' departure. She waited for them to digest the night's information and steeled herself for whatever reaction it would solicit.

Rory spoke first, but on a professional rather than a personal basis. "Do you want to press charges, Caleb?"

Caleb shook his head. He probably didn't want any further ties to Robbie. "All I want is peace to get my home restored."

His home. My home. Our home.

"He should pay for the damage, at least." Her father's suggestion brought mumbled agreement from everyone.

The clock on the mantelpiece ticked through another lull of silence.

Mia took up the challenge. "Are we actually going to discuss the fact that I am with Caleb? That I'm moving in with him?"

"What's to discuss? You two are together. Go be happy." Trust Rory to make it sound all so simple.

"Mum?" She went straight to the source of her main worry. Her mother would never be his number one fan and she wouldn't be surprised if she blamed him for tarnishing Robbie's halo too.

"Do you love him, Mia?" She got straight to the point, never minding that Caleb was within hearing distance.

"Yes. I love him." Mia reached out to rest a hand on his knee, declaring it loud and clear.

Her mother gave a resigned sigh. Preferable to the tears and dramatics she'd grown used to. "I guess I'm not much of a judge of character, going by the choice I made for you."

Mia's heart hammered, threatening to burst through her ribs. She was putting everything on the line here — her family, her security, her heart — all for Caleb. But he was worth it. Nothing frightened her as much as the thought of losing him. They belonged together. They both knew it, even if they'd been too stubborn to admit it up until now.

"And you love Mia?" Her mother asked Caleb the question Mia feared the answer to most. 'No' meant a broken heart. 'Yes' meant a giant leap into the unknown. Either way her life would change forever.

"Mr and Mrs Blake, I love your daughter with all my heart. Even though she kinda sprung it on me too, I'd love nothing more than to have her move in with me. When the place is habitable, of course." Caleb placed his hand on hers and jump-started her breathing, which she'd forgotten to do since he'd started to speak. It didn't matter that the first time he'd said he loved her had been in front of her family, at least she now knew for sure.

"So, we'll have our little girl for a while longer at least." The shine of tears in her father's eyes startled her. In contrast to her mother, he didn't normally share his feelings so openly.

"It's not like I'm emigrating abroad or anything. I'm only moving up the road." Mia swallowed the lump in her throat, unprepared for this level of emotion. Yes, she'd expected drama, but this almost silent acceptance was both a surprise and a relief. She couldn't help but wonder if Rory had cleared the way beforehand.

"We know. But over these last years you've been so lost drifting from one dead-end job to another with no clear goal. Now you seem to know exactly what you want. It's almost as though you don't need us anymore." Even her mother now shed a tear, and not in that guilt-trip way she usually employed. Mia knew they were a genuine display of her fears.

"I will always need you. Just in a different way." She was already looking forward to her new life and finding her way in the world with Caleb by her side.

"If you hurt her, I'll use your hide as a foot warmer." Her father let his wolf warn Caleb, his eyes glowing and his claws tapping the arm of his chair. A serious display of alpha male. The Blakes didn't shift in front of anyone.

"He knows the score. I've already threatened him with dismemberment." Rory joined forces to try to end their relationship before it had begun.

"Hey! What's with the chest-beating, people? He said he loves me. What more do you want?" There was nothing to spoil a precious moment better than your father and brother snarling like a pack of wild dogs.

"Don't worry. You have my permission to kick my arse if I ever step out of line." Caleb took their threats in his stride, allowing Mia to unclench her fists.

"Does that go for me too?" Now that the law was laid down, she joined in the banter.

"You, sweetheart, have permission to do anything you want to my arse." Caleb wiggled an eyebrow in his dastardly villain manner, leaving her family recoiling.

"Oh, now that's too much information."

"You've overstepped the line there, Caleb."

"There are some things better kept private."

It broke the ice to send them all into delicious echoes of laughter. Although he would always be rough around the edges, she knew her family would soon accept him as one of their own.

* * * *

"I think that went better than expected." Caleb held Mia in his arms, out on the porch of her family home.

"I particularly liked the bit where you said you loved me." She snuggled into his chest and listened to the steady beat of his heart.

"Really? I preferred the part when Robbie's mother slapped him around the head and he cried like a girl."

She slapped his chest. "Take that back."

"Okay. Okay. Him calling me a 'fucking moron' was pretty special too."

Her fingers found his nipple, rigid in the cold air, and tweaked it.

"Ouch! I'm only joking." He tilted her chin up and kissed her hard until she forgave him. "I love you, and I love that you love me. Okay?"

"Good. I wouldn't want to have to give you that arse kicking so soon." She reached around to squeeze his tight butt cheeks.

"As much as I want you right here, right now, I think that might be pushing my luck with your parents." He nuzzled into her hair and trailed his hands down her spine and over her backside.

"We could always make a run for it." Mia let go of his peachy arse and started to unzip her little black dress.

"I like your thinking." Caleb followed her down the steps, unbuttoning his jeans and toeing off his boots.

In the silver ribbons of moonlight, the dark silhouettes of two wolves streaked across the Irish countryside nipping at each other's heels. Neither one straying too far from the other, they ran towards their future, together.

Epilogue

"Sorry I'm late. It's been one of those days." Naomi bustled through the front door, shaking water from her umbrella over the floor.

"No worries. I know you're not about to flee the country without her." Mia led her through to the playroom where Emily was studiously colouring at the table. The last of her charges to leave before she could lock up for the night.

"Hello, sweetheart."

"Mummy!" Emily jumped up and came charging towards them. Mia dodged out of the way as Emily ran full pelt into Naomi's arms.

"I can't tell you how glad I am that I can pick her up and be home again in five minutes. Have I told you how much I love you, even though you left me one brilliant barmaid down?" Naomi thanked her for the hundredth time as she wiggled Emily into her coat.

Mia smiled. "Yes, you have. Every night when you collect her."

She had Naomi and her daughter to thank for putting her on this path in the first place. The time she'd spent with Emily had started her interest in doing the childcare course, and now here she was with her own fully staffed crèche right in the middle of the village. Mr Carson, of course, also contributed to the success of The Cub Club. His guilt over his son's actions made sure she received a generous discount on the rent.

"Well, you're a lifesaver. Now, I hope Caleb is picking you up so you can go home and put your feet up." Naomi slipped back into her bossy role even though Mia hadn't worked for her in over a year.

"He'll be here soon, but no early night for me, I'm afraid. In case you've forgotten, he's playing at The Dog tonight." No matter how uncomfortable she felt right now, she wouldn't miss one of his gigs for the world.

Naomi buttoned herself up to face the stormy night. "You look after yourself and I'll see you in the morning."

Mia waved them off at the door, just as Caleb drove up to meet her. It still made her laugh that he'd swapped his bad boy bike for the practical SUV. "Are you two ready to roll?" He planted a kiss on her lips, and one on her swollen belly.

"Give me five minutes to lock up." She went around, closing doors and switching off the lights. Caleb picked up the crayons and paper lying on the carpet, knowing full well that she could no longer bend down to pick them up.

"I wish you would make an appearance soon, so I can see my feet again," she said out loud to her bump.

Caleb smoothed his hands over her round belly and added his request to see Junior. "We can't wait to meet you, little one."

Mia pulled him into a hug, touched by his support throughout the whole pregnancy. They hadn't planned for it to happen when they had just been getting on their feet. The crèche was still a new business and the money Caleb made from renting his land to nearby farmers wasn't a fortune, but they were both excited about welcoming this new life they'd created.

"Do you think I'll make a good dad?" he'd asked Mia once they'd stopped dancing around the room waving the pregnancy test. The question was inevitable given his relationship with his own father, but she knew him better than he knew himself.

"You'll be a fantastic father." The months since she'd moved in with him had been the happiest of her life. She didn't even have to look at Robbie's smarmy face now that his father had packed him off to their Dublin branch of the company in disgrace. Having Caleb's baby was the thick sweet icing on the perfect cake.

"I love you, Mia." Caleb brought her back to the present as his lips caressed hers in a kiss every bit as passionate as their first.

"I love you too." He still made her breathless with his every touch.

Caleb ran his fingers through his already messy blond locks and she could tell he had something on his mind. "I was going to do this at the pub, but it seems right to do it here. Alone."

"Do what?" A shooting pain caught her unawares and temporarily distracted her from Caleb's strange behaviour. She just wanted him to get a move on so she could sit down by the fire in the pub.

He knelt down, and stood up again. What the hell? Another pain ripped through her, making her wince.

"I'm not sure how to do this, Mia."

"Well, could you hurry up? Pregnant woman standing here." A strange tugging sensation in her abdomen zapped the last of her patience.

"Will you marry me?"

A flood gushed between her legs and soaked the floor. "Oh, shit!"

Caleb stopped fumbling in his pocket long enough to give her the puppy eyes. "Oh shit, no? Or, oh shit, yes?"

"I mean, oh shit, my waters have broken. Can you ask me again when I'm less preoccupied?" The romance of the moment was definitely lost in the puddle at her feet.

He looked at her sodden shoes and froze.

"Er, earth to Caleb. We need to move. Like now!"

"Right. Right." He took her arm as she waddled to the front door, and helped her out into the front seat of the car.

"Do you think you could lock the place up for me?" She pointed out the front door lying wide open. *And I thought I would be the basket case when this time came.*

* * * *

Caleb thought his heart would burst with pride as he stood in the delivery room looking at the two women in his life. He cradled baby Sophie in his arms, so smitten that he no longer noticed the pain where Mia had crushed his fingers during the birth. "She's beautiful, like her mother."

"Her father's not so bad either." Mia reached out from the bed, looking for her cuddle, and he gingerly handed over his precious bundle.

He would never have believed that he could have all this. That he could be a family man and enjoy the contentment of a stable home. There was just one thing missing.

"You didn't answer my question earlier."

Mia tore her eyes away from her mini-me and looked at him with the same love-filled gaze. "Maybe you should ask it again. I promise to listen this time."

"Is it safe to get down on one knee now?"

"Yeah. The flood warning has passed now." Her smile made him fall in love with her all over again.

He pulled his chair over to the bed where Mia lay with their daughter in her arms, the picture of his happiness. "Mia Blake, will you make me the happiest wolf in the hills and marry me?" He produced the diamond solitaire ring he'd misplaced earlier in all the excitement.

"As long as you don't expect me to do any of that obeying crap, yes, I will marry you, Caleb Jackson."

He slid the ring onto her finger, certain that his life was only just beginning.

THE WOLF ON THE RUN

Dedication

Thanks to everyone who bought 'The Wolf on the Hill' and asked me to write Rory's story. I didn't take much convincing to be honest. I've had a soft spot for him since the beginning! My gratitude also goes to my lovely editor, Sue, whose enthusiasm is infectious and makes the writing process so much easier.

Chapter One

"Thanks for stepping in here, Mia. It looks like we have a rush on today." Naomi squeezed past her friend to serve a stream of new customers at the bar. Although Mia was no longer her employee, she'd volunteered to give a helping hand during her lunch break from her childcare centre.

"It might have something to do with this." Mia stopped pulling pints long enough to grab the newspaper out of Rory's hands.

"Hey!"

Mia ignored her brother's protest across the counter and thumbed through the pages until she found what she was looking for.

"There you go." With a tap of her finger, she directed Naomi to an article taking up half the page.

'Good food, cold beer and a warm welcome at The Wild Dog'

The headline topped a photograph of her pub. Naomi's blood ran cold as she scanned paragraph after paragraph. There it was in black and white — *'Licensee, Naomi Duffy...'*

The words swam together as her world came crashing down around her.

"It's great publicity, isn't it? Rory has a contact at the newspaper." Mia carried on serving as though Naomi hadn't just been delivered, gift wrapped, to the Devil himself.

"You did this?" Naomi spun around to face the well-meaning policeman she'd been trying to avoid these past months.

His dark chocolate eyes widened at the harsh tone of her voice. "I just recommended the place to a mate —"

"For once in your life, Rory, I wish you'd mind your own bloody business!" The stunned look on his face blurred as tears marred her vision. She slapped the newspaper into his broad chest and made a hasty exit before she caused any more of a scene.

After her few years of freedom here, the walls of the pub suddenly became her prison. Keeping her trapped until the O'Connells found her. After reverting back to her maiden name and moving to Northern Ireland, she'd tried to minimise the disruption for her daughter's sake, and prayed they would never cross the border to find her. She'd done her best to keep her anonymity, avoiding social network sites and generally staying under the radar. This small piece of publicity could potentially seal her fate.

Like the hunted animal she now was, Naomi scrabbled for her freedom through the back door. Doubled over outside the cellar doors, she fought to breathe as fear clawed from the inside out. Should she run? This was her livelihood. Olcan Hills was the only home Emily had ever known. Yet, if she stayed and they came for her daughter…

Naomi retched at the very thought of the consequences.

"Okay. Let's have this out." She heard Rory a fraction of a second before he grabbed her by the wrist and yanked her upright.

"This isn't the time." He was lucky she didn't puke on his shiny black shoes.

"You're right. The time should've been about ten months ago when I kissed you." He nudged her chin up with his finger, forcing her to look at him. It would probably be better for her health if he kept up the brutish act instead of reverting back to his typical kind-hearted self.

"Don't—" The nausea dissipated, leaving that all too familiar ache in her heart she experienced every time she saw him.

"Don't what? Talk to you? Try to help you? Kiss you?" He dropped his gaze to her mouth and her poor heart took another hammering.

The memory of that sweet kiss was forever imprinted on her lips. The tenderness in that brief moment almost made up for the long time she'd spent denying herself any happiness. But nothing could come of it.

"We're friends, Rory. What happened was a mistake. We simply got caught up in our friends' joy after the birth of their baby." Emotions had been running high all around when they'd welcomed baby Sophie into the world, with proud Uncle Rory and honorary Aunt Naomi. She'd simply let her guard down and acted on the simmering attraction during a friendly hug. One kiss couldn't erase her past, and she wouldn't take a chance on getting involved with someone when she had so much at stake.

"I've spent long enough hanging back, waiting until you're ready to accept there's something between us.

For some reason you seem determined to keep me at arm's length."

There weren't many men like Rory Blake willing to give her the space to work out her feelings. It made what she had to do even worse.

"If you've spent nearly a year mooning over a peck on the lips, you really ought to get yourself a life." She shook off the emotional attachment with a toss of her dark hair and walked away, pretending her heart wasn't breaking in two. He might hate her for the cruelty now, but ultimately she was saving him from a shitload of hurt down the road. After all, she'd damned near killed him already.

The cannonball of hurt, which fired into his gut, almost felled Rory's six foot two frame. It took a moment for him to get his breath back after the tiny brunette's torrent of ire. He could lash out in similar fashion and tell her she meant nothing to him, but where was the point in lying?

"I don't know what happened to make you change the way you feel about me, but I know we have something."

He made another grab for her and spun her back around. A lock of her hair fell across her big brown eyes and he was halfway to brushing it away when he caught himself. He let his hand drift aimlessly to his side, leaving her hair to shield her partially from view.

"I won't beg. Just know I'm here for you."

Rory sucked up the last of his dignity and released her. He'd waited this long for her, he guessed a little while longer wouldn't make much difference. *And if she still doesn't want me?* The steady pace he'd started towards his car slowed and he fumbled with his keys.

The enormity of Naomi's rejection hit him as he collapsed into the driver's seat. She was right. He was beyond sad. What was the first thing he'd said when she'd told him to back off? 'I'm here for you'. Loser.

He groaned and released his frustration on the steering wheel with the palm of his hand. With a serious need to escape his humiliation, he over revved the engine and left the object of his unrequited love behind in a cloud of dust.

* * * *

"What have you got for me, Juliette?" Dressed in his freshly pressed uniform, Rory strode into the station.

"Evening, Constable Blake." The flash of pink warming the pretty receptionist's pale complexion was the first thing to bring a smile to his face all day.

Since she'd started the job six months ago, she hadn't hidden her crush on him very well. He'd found it flattering of course, but he'd been too caught up in his own infatuation to act on it. Well, there was nothing standing in the way of a little flirtation now, was there?

"Nothing much. Only a couple of calls about anti-social behaviour out by the Kerr place." She handed the details to him, and let her hand brush against his a tad longer than necessary.

"Thanks, sweetheart." He couldn't resist bringing that sweet glow back to her cheeks. It did his ego good to see he wasn't totally repellent to the opposite sex.

"If there's nothing else I can do for you, I guess I'll be on my way." Rory's cheeky wink solicited a coy giggle to boost him on his way. His loyalty to Naomi thus far had meant living like a monk for far too long.

He got into his patrol car, glad he at least had his work to stop him from falling into a pit of despair. On the other hand, the long, lonely drive around the Olcan hills gave him way too much time for introspection.

The dark endless night encroaching on him pretty much reflected his life. Empty, with no glimmer of light to guide him. He was actually glad when the headlights picked out the band of miscreants running amok at the side of the road. It saved him from drowning in a sea of self-pity.

Blue lights flashing, he pulled the car over onto the grass verge. Rory lifted his cap from the passenger seat and fixed it on his head before he approached the group. The teenagers banded together, unsuccessfully trying to hide several tins of beer behind their backs.

"Seriously, guys. You of all people should realise how good my eyesight is in the dark." Being a wolf shifter in the Police Service of Northern Ireland had its advantages. He reached behind the tallest kid to retrieve the evidence.

"Sorry, Rory." Jamie Frazer was the obvious ringleader, in and out of trouble since his dad died just over a year ago.

Rory cocked an eyebrow, demanding a fraction more respect.

"Sorry, Officer." Somehow he managed to sound even more condescending. The rest sniggered, following his lead.

This wasn't the evening to piss Rory Blake off. He opened the can and emptied the contents at the boys' feet.

"And the rest." He stopped short of a growl, but the low rumble of his voice was authoritative enough to make them comply. Can after can of beer followed, much to the horror of the underage drinkers.

"That's such a waste." Jamie mourned the loss while Rory poured his day's troubles into a satisfying puddle.

"If you prefer I can escort each of you home and report your activities to your folks?"

This time they did him the courtesy of looking shamefaced, staring down at their dirty trainers as the forbidden alcohol seeped into the countryside. "No thanks."

"In that case, keep the noise down, stop annoying the neighbours, and I won't have cause to trouble your parents. And, Jamie, I'm guessing your brother wouldn't take too kindly to having another visit from me?"

"No, sir."

Rory hoped the warning would do the trick. He knew Jamie's older brother had enough on his plate trying to keep the family together. After all, Rory had done his own fair share of stand-in parenting for Mia on his workaholic mother and father's behalf.

Now that he seemed to have reached an understanding with the teen tearaway, Rory removed his cap and tucked it under his arm, switching into his role as Alpha. "I get you're going through a lot of changes right now, getting used to your shifter sides. Try and channel your energies into something other than making trouble. As your Alpha I can turn a blind eye if you want to shift and run wild in the woods. But, as a police officer, I can't stand by and let you break the law. Do you understand me?"

"Yes." The collective mumble was enough reassurance for Rory to move on.

As he left them behind in his rear-view mirror, he knew that incident would most likely be the most he had to deal with tonight. Out here in the sticks he didn't usually encounter anything more exciting than petty theft or alcohol related incidents. If he worked closer to Belfast he'd be in the heart of city life, with the added danger of the paramilitary factions. Of course, there was always the option of transferring to the south of Ireland, or even across the water to the mainland.

In over a decade he'd never actively sought promotion in the force. His job here in Olcan Hills suited him. It meant he was close enough to keep an eye on Mia, and he could combine his police role with being Alpha, keeping the pack safe from outsiders. Now, though, Mia had Caleb to look after her, the community largely looked after itself and Naomi had made it clear she didn't want him in her life.

Maybe, just once, he should focus on his own future and the one thing he had left in his life — his job.

Chapter Two

"I am so glad to be able to put my feet up." Mia plopped onto the sofa beside Naomi while their girls played happily nearby.

"How's work going?" Naomi knew exactly how hard it was to run a business and raise a child at the same time. At least Mia had Caleb by her side.

"Knackering to say the least." Mia's laugh lit up her whole face and she didn't look the tiniest bit worn out. Unlike Naomi, who hadn't managed a full night's sleep since the newspaper fallout.

"You know, if you'd have told me three years ago I would be settled down with Caleb Jackson of all people I'd never have believed it. And we have this little one to keep us on our toes too." Mia grabbed a bib from the arm of the chair to dab at the corners of Sophie's toothy grin.

"Teething again?" Naomi spotted the dribbly signs on the baby's once white dress.

"Yep." Mia left her daughter with a kiss on the forehead.

"It seems like only yesterday Emily was that little and she'll be starting school next year." These last years living in relative peace seemed a lifetime away from the dark days of her pregnancy. Naomi shuddered and blocked her mind to those images that were the stuff of nightmares.

"Are you cold? I can put the heat on if you want?" Mia made to get up.

"No. I'm fine. Someone must have walked over my grave." Usually words spoken in jest, they were closer to home in Naomi's case. Only the life growing inside her had given her the strength to fight at that time, and escape to Olcan Hills.

Mia followed her gaze to the two girls. "They're like chalk and cheese, aren't they?"

"Absolutely." Emily's dark curls were a contrast to Sophie's angelic blonde tresses, and where Mia's daughter was bubbly, Emily had the same serious countenance as her mother.

Naomi couldn't help but wonder if she'd passed on her stresses over the years, or if the difference between the two girls was something more...genetic.

"Have you ever noticed a difference between shifter and non-shifter tots at work?"

"Perhaps their senses are more developed, but that's about it. They're all boisterous at that age so it's hard to tell them apart. You're not worrying about Emily changing already, are you? You've a few years to go yet." Mia patted her arm but it didn't do anything to ease Naomi's concerns. With Emily's parentage, she couldn't be sure when, or even what, her daughter would shift into. Not when she was only half wolf shifter.

She gave a half-hearted laugh to cover her secret fear. "I'm a mum. It's our job to worry."

The sound of the front door opening stopped Naomi from spilling out all her secrets to the only friend she had.

"Caleb? Is that you?" Both Mia and Sophie turned towards the door and Naomi could see the excitement written all over their faces.

Sometimes Naomi envied their home life. Especially alone at night when she was too afraid of the dark to turn the lights off.

"Yes, love." He popped his blond head through the door to say hello.

"Will you stick the kettle on for us?" Mia batted her eyelashes at the obviously smitten Caleb.

"Yes, mistress." He bowed before going over to pull a babbling Sophie into his arms. "Hey, wee woman. Why doesn't Daddy take you into the kitchen and find you something to eat? Do you want to come and get some juice too, Emily?"

The dolls' tea party was abandoned in favour of real goodies as the children went willingly with Caleb.

"You have him well trained." Naomi wallowed in the scene of domestic bliss unfolding before her eyes.

"Ah, I think it's the baby who's tamed him from the local hellion into Mr Mom. But yeah, I'm one lucky lady."

"Yes, you are." Naomi wondered what her life would've been like if she'd had a partner to look after her and Emily, or if she'd ever have one in the future. As things stood, even if someone wanted that position in her life, she would never risk opening herself up for more hurt. She couldn't risk giving away her heart only to have it broken again further down the line. And, if her nightmares came true, some day she might have to go back on the run. Only one person had almost fooled her into thinking she could have her fairy tale ending here in the hills and she'd made damn sure he wouldn't come back for seconds.

"How are things with you and my brother?" Mia hopped on board her train of thought—The Rory Express, the fastest way to Heartbreak City, stopping at Torment Town and Regret Central.

"We're friends, that's all." All they could ever be.

"Yeah? You didn't look too friendly yesterday when you were beating him around the head with a newspaper. He was only trying to help. That's what he does." His loyal sister wasn't telling Naomi anything she didn't already know, but without being privy to her reasons she realised the events made her look like a bit of a bitch.

"I'll apologise when I see him again. I'm just not used to having people butting into my business." That one simple act of lamented kindness might have killed any hopes of her and Emily staying here for good.

"That's Rory for you. A big ol' butthead." Despite the strong bond with her brother, as diplomatic as ever, Mia didn't appear to take sides. Even though Naomi was clearly the one in the wrong.

"Tea's up, ladies." Caleb came back into the room carrying two mismatched mugs, with Sophie crawling behind him and Emily carrying a plate of biscuits.

"Thank you, waitress." Naomi helped herself to a much needed chocolate boost.

"So, Naomi, did Mia tell you the news?" Caleb dropped down to help Sophie to her feet, holding her chubby little hands as she took wobbly steps towards her mother.

"No." Mia frowned her disapproval at him.

"What news?" Obviously he'd stuck his foot in it, but Naomi was keen to have something else to focus on other than her own problems.

Mia directed another dirty look at Caleb before she spoke again. "We finally set a date."

"For the wedding? Congratulations!" With happy tears pricking her eyes, Naomi grabbed her friend for a hug. "Congratulations!" she said again, releasing Mia to embrace Caleb too.

"I was getting around to asking you this in private, but would you be my maid of honour?" As the biggest smile spread over Mia's face, she appeared to have forgiven Caleb for spilling the news first.

"I, er..." A range of emotions and scenarios ran through Naomi's head. Of course she was ecstatic to be asked to be part of their big day, but there was always that dark cloud hanging over her. What if she had no choice but to up sticks and move again before then?

"And we want Emily to be our flower girl."

Emily's eyes lit up at the offer of being princess for a day, meaning a refusal was out of the question.

"We'd love to, wouldn't we, Em?" Bless her, it was more excitement than the child had ever known judging by her nodding dog impression.

"How does the first of November suit you?" Caleb let out another sliver of information, this time with Mia's apparent approval.

That meant another couple of months of looking over her shoulder for Naomi, but the wedding meant the decision about leaving was taken out of her hands for the time being.

"It's great. I'm so happy for you both." She was genuinely delighted Caleb and Mia were finally making their relationship official when they'd seemed so shy of commitment at the beginning of their badly concealed relationship.

"And how are things between you and the big guy?" Caleb gave her the distinct impression she and Rory had been the topic of much conversation in the Jackson-Blake household.

Naomi tried not to lose her cool. Why did people suddenly think she and Rory were having a *thing* and they'd had some sort of lover's tiff? *We had one bloody kiss!* "Fine."

"Great. 'Cause we wouldn't want any friction on the big day. I'm going to ask him to be my best man."

That familiar sickness swept over her, as she anticipated spending time in his company. At a time when she needed as much distance from him as possible, her so-called friends had made damn sure she was tied to him for the foreseeable future. *Great! Now I've conjured up an image of a naked Constable Blake swinging his handcuffs at me.*

Sometimes Naomi wondered if life would be a hell of a lot simpler if she'd just kept running.

* * * *

With the usual trouble spots dutifully checked and found quiet, Rory's night was giving him far too much time to wallow in his own thoughts. He could see the light from Mia and Caleb's cottage up on the hill, and suddenly had the urge for company.

It might do him some good to chew the fat with Caleb over a coffee. Besides, if anything serious came up, Juliette would make sure he was on it.

The warm fuzzies he had when he started towards the house started to frost over when he saw Naomi's dark blue Mini parked outside. A U-turn in the middle of the lane would be too obvious, not to mention immature. So, he pulled up, took a deep breath and braced himself to face the woman who'd so callously ripped his heart out only a matter of hours ago.

"Am I glad to see you, mate. I'm out numbered four to one here," Caleb answered the door with Sophie slung around waist and Emily clinging to his leg.

"Rory!" The normally shy Emily let go of Caleb to launch herself at Rory.

"Hey, kiddo." He swung her up into his arms, thankful he'd stowed his belt and gun in the car before he'd come in.

"Rory, Auntie Mia says I can be her flower girl and I can pick my own dress," she chattered away, obviously excited about it.

"Really?" He cocked an eyebrow at Caleb and waited for confirmation. It didn't come as much of a surprise to hear his sister was getting married. To all intents and purposes they were living as husband and wife here anyway. But it would have been nice to have heard the news first-hand.

"I'm saying nothing in case I land myself in the shit again. Talk to your sister." Caleb closed the front door before letting Rory into the living room.

Although he knew she was on the other side of the door, the sight of Naomi curled up on the settee made his stomach drop like a stone. He turned his attention to Mia perched beside her.

"I hear you're getting hitched, sis."

Caleb shrugged his shoulders. "It wasn't me this time."

"Sorry, Rory. We were going to tell you we'd set the date." Mia peeled Sophie from Caleb's arms and the sleepy child buried into her mother's bosom.

"No worries. Congratulations." With Emily still in his arms, he leant down to kiss his sister on the cheek.

"You too, mate." He straightened up to congratulate Caleb too.

"I'll settle for a handshake if you don't mind." Caleb slapped his hand into Rory's in a manly exchange of good wishes.

"I'm sure the folks will be every bit as happy as I am for you too." Although they'd never said so, Rory knew his parents didn't approve of their daughter living in sin. In his old fashioned idea of romance and family, he thought it would also be good for his niece to have her parents married.

"Well, we didn't get off to a great start, but I'd like to think I'd won Gayle and Eddie over since then." That infamous dinner where Caleb had alluded to being a male gigolo just to stick one to the snobby contingent of the Blake family would go down in history.

"Ah, you're one of the family now, Caleb. I think giving them Sophie to dote on earned you some much needed brownie points." It amazed Rory to see how much time his parents wanted to spend with their granddaughter when they could never spare any for their own children. He supposed it was their way of making amends, but would they ever get the same chance to make it up to him?

"I'm glad you think that way, big man. I want you to be my best man."

"I'd love to." Caleb's offer managed to stick a plaster over Rory's damaged pride.

"No wild stag night with strippers, or shaved eyebrows, mind." If the look on Mia's face was anything to go by she was only half-joking.

"As if I would dream of doing such a thing." Rory winked at Caleb to reassure him he'd receive a fitting send off into married life.

"We're counting on you and Naomi to help us get organised over the next few weeks, and to keep our over-bearing parentals at bay. Naomi's agreed to be my maid of honour." Mia didn't rise to the teasing and instead threw back the curveball.

Rory slid a glance over at Naomi, who seemed determined not to make eye contact with him. More than likely she wasn't thrilled about being partnered with him so soon after shooting him down. Rory had mixed feelings. He didn't want his nose rubbed in the fact he couldn't have her, and yet it gave him reason to be close to her again. He suspected he had something of a masochist streak going on.

"I think we need to get sleepy head here up to bed, and then we can celebrate the good news." Caleb nodded towards the snoring baby.

"Not for me. I'm on duty. I should really get back out there." Rory handed his Emily shaped package over to Naomi. "See you later, missus."

"Night, night, Rory." The child gave him a last hug that told him she was every bit as fond of him as he was of her. Pity Ms Duffy senior didn't express that same sentiment.

"We should get going too." Still refusing to look at him, Naomi got to her feet and hoisted handbag and daughter onto her small frame.

"I'm sure Rory will see you out, while we get this one up to bed. Night all." Without a hint of subtlety Mia made her exit trailing Caleb behind.

"Night." Naomi didn't hang around. She said her goodbyes and was out of the door quicker than a greyhound out of a trap.

Undeterred, Rory soon caught up and opened the car door so she could manoeuvre Emily into her car seat.

"Thanks." She gave him a grateful smile but was already edging farther towards her escape.

"So are you talking to me then?" He needed to at least get back on speaking terms with her.

"Of course. I'm sorry about some of the things I said. I'm a bit stressed, that's all." With the interior car light shining on her face, dark circles underlined her dark brown eyes.

His first instinct was to question what had her so worried. And which things she regretted saying. He didn't push her though. Sometimes Naomi was more like a skittish deer than a fierce wolf. One step too close and she bolted.

"Are we still friends?" In this small community it made more sense than trying to avoid each other.

"Friends." Her genuine smile was enough for him to fall in love with her all over again. He'd known for quite a while how strong his feelings were for Naomi Duffy and now there was bugger all he could do about it. Unrequited love sucked.

Chapter Three

"Thanks for doing this, Caleb." Naomi watched Emily skip happily into the cottage.

"No problem. Sure, I'm minding Sophie here anyway. Besides, I'll be glad of the break from Bridezilla." Caleb earned himself a clip round the ear from Mia.

"Oi! I'd rather be talking about our upcoming nuptials than bore people whining on about an old motorbike." The smiles never left the couple's faces through their banter. Although they both had feisty personalities, Naomi couldn't remember a time Caleb and Mia had seriously argued. Except when he'd first come to town and everything he had done had appeared to wind Mia up.

"That T-Bird was my pride and joy. I miss it." The dramatic sigh didn't fool Naomi. Caleb had voluntarily sold it to fix up the cottage and put down some roots in the community. There was no way he'd give up all this now for some old motorbike.

"Well, now you've got me and Sophie, your baby bird. So get over it already." Mia dropped a kiss on his nose and closed the front door.

"Are you sure he can manage by himself?" Worry came naturally to Naomi, even though Caleb and Mia were the only people she trusted with her daughter. And Rory, of course.

"I reckon he'll rope my brother in somewhere along the line to help. It's Saturday afternoon, I'm not there to nag, and there's probably football on the telly. Sounds like a perfect day for male bonding if you ask me." Mia didn't display any anxiety over leaving her daughter. Another symbol of the security they had in their perfect family unit.

Naomi opened the car door and plopped into the seat with a sigh. "Can we handle one day without any responsibilities where all we have to think about is dresses and where to have coffee?" She was starting to look forward to it.

"Bring it on." Mia clipped in her seatbelt and sat poised for Naomi to put their arses in gear.

* * * *

Naomi didn't spend much time in Belfast and wasn't used to city driving, so she parked the car in the Titanic Quarter. "It's a bit of a walk to the main shopping route, but it's better than getting caught up in traffic at least."

"No worries. We can do a bit of sightseeing on the way. I haven't been here in ages." Mia pointed out all the new buildings transforming the old docks with a thriving new tourist attraction.

"Me neither." In her attempt to remain low key, Naomi had stuck to the rural highways and byways. As a result she'd missed out on a lot.

They crossed the bridge over the River Lagan, a light mist spraying their faces as they walked.

"Where to first?" A frothy cappuccino would hit the spot for Naomi, but this was Mia's day.

The bride-to-be pulled out her purse and waved her magic card. "Have plastic, will shop."

They did some window shopping in Ann Street and Royal Avenue, bypassing the camera toting tourists at City Hall to arrive at their first bridal boutique. The over the top white meringue dress on display in the window wasn't Mia's style, but it was as good a place to start as any.

Practically bouncing with excitement, Mia pushed the door open. The chimes as they entered summoned a shop assistant to hover nearby.

"Look at all the dresses." The rails of white and ivory silk drew Mia like a dieter to a doughnut factory. She flipped through hangers, until Naomi swore she got sequin blindness.

Mia's hand stilled. "This is real."

Tears pricked at Naomi's eyes as she nodded. She'd missed all this excitement in the lead up to her own wedding. Fearing their parents' reaction to their union, she and Kian had been forced to marry in secret with none of the frills Mia now revelled in.

"Can I help you?" They didn't hear the pinch-faced assistant approach, her stilettos silent in the thick carpet. She stared down her turned-up nose to regard Mia and Naomi with disdain.

Naomi's hackles rose. "We're just looking. Thank you."

"When is the wedding?" Frosty Knickers addressed Mia directly.

"November." Mia's sparkle gradually dimmed with every second they remained under scrutiny.

"Well, dear, I think you'd need to do more than look."

It took every ounce of Naomi's usually impeccable self-control not to knock the bitch over and tear her throat out for spoiling Mia's experience. The wolf baiter took the dress from Mia's hand and hung it back on the rail. She dusted the plastic covering of the wedding dress as if it had been soiled in the two seconds Mia had held it.

"I'm not even sure we have anything suitable for you here." She looked Mia up and down with an obvious aversion to her jeans and sweater combo.

Naomi's blood started to boil as her friend was treated like a social reject in the middle of the store. Money might be tight these days for Caleb and Mia, but it certainly didn't give anyone the right to judge, or ruin their big day.

Since hooking up with Caleb and breaking free from her parents' hold, Mia was more than capable of fighting her own battles. But, perhaps her hormones hadn't quite settled after having the baby, as she stood and took one insult after another. Naomi wasn't so inclined.

With her wolf clawing to be released, she stood between Mia and the bitch. "You're right. This place isn't for the likes of us."

Frosty knickers nodded her approval.

"Why would you give commission to a stuck up bitch like this who probably hasn't been laid in centuries and wants to take out her frustration on happy brides such as yourself, Mia?"

Mia's snigger met her foe's gasp.

"You can't talk to me like that." This woman didn't know when to keep her trap shut.

"And you can't get away with talking to customers the way you just did." Naomi did something she didn't usually do in public and let her wolf have its moment. She tapped one long nail on the assistant's name badge.

"Celia, is it? Well, Celia, I'll let you live...this time. But in future watch who you're talking to. It can come back to bite you on the arse. Literally." Naomi gave her a brief flash of her wolf eyes, and judging by the look on her face it was almost enough to make Celia piss herself.

Toying with her prey also proved a mood enhancer for Mia as she joined in the She-Wolf offensive to growl a warning. "I don't hear you apologising."

"I-I'm sorry if I offended you," Celia stumbled.

Their cover well and truly blown, Naomi knew they couldn't hang around. "I think it's better all around if we take our business elsewhere."

She held out her arm and Mia hooked hers through it. They left the shop almost skipping up the high street, ignoring Celia's collapse into the nearest chair.

"Rory would kill us if he knew what we'd just done." At least Mia was smiling again.

"She deserved it, but let's make a pact never to tell anyone. Especially your brother." They didn't need Rory to lecture them on the perils of exposing the general public to their shifter sides. Sometimes Naomi's temper got the better of her. Like when she'd gone off at Rory in the car park. Attack was the best part of her defence.

"I quite enjoyed freaking the old bat out. Maybe we should become some sort of vigilante squad scaring the crap out of holier-than-thou bints like Celia." Mia's rebellious streak needed capping before they both ended up on the front of *The Belfast Telegraph*.

"No one will believe her, so best not take any chances, eh? Now, I think I need my shot of caffeine before we try that shopping lark again." A day with Mia was never going to be boring.

* * * *

After a welcome break for coffee and double choc chip muffins, the rest of their afternoon went relatively smoothly. Mia found the perfect dress in a vintage store off Ann Street—a simple, white strapless gown with diamanté detail across the bust and a short train. Understated but beautiful.

Naomi's strappy silver dress was on sale in a high street store and they teamed it with a faux fur stole to stop her from freezing her bits off in the height of winter.

Shoe shopping was a simple task, both opting for kitten heels for practical purposes. They decided Emily deserved her own day to choose her outfit and resolved to set another date aside to treat her. The thought of having a mother-daughter trip to the city like any other normal family was an alien concept.

Naomi feigned a yawn and rubbed the back of her neck. "If you're done, do you mind if we head back?"

"Sure." Mia didn't hide her disappointment but after shopping and lunching, Naomi's thoughts had returned to her daughter.

She'd never taken a chance where her safety was concerned and she wasn't about to start now when Kian's family could be out there, waiting to pounce.

* * * *

"I should've known you had an ulterior motive for asking me over." Rory took in the scene of devastation before him—the toys strewn all around, the dirty dishes and the red-faced infant squirming in Caleb's arms.

"'The girls are out,' he said. 'Come over and watch the match,' he said. I don't remember volunteering for babysitting." Rory should have known his future bro-in-law's game, he'd fallen it for it enough.

"Yay, girls. Uncle Rory's here." Caleb ignored the sarcasm to call Emily and Sophie.

Where's Naomi?

As if reading his mind, Caleb added, "Naomi went dress shopping with Mia."

"And they left you holding the babies?" Rory wondered what life-changing event had occurred for Naomi to venture into the city and leave her daughter in the hands of, well, Caleb.

"Now it's you holding the baby." Caleb grinned and handed over the squirming Sophie.

Rory cuddled her close, the heat of her skin searing him through his thin white cotton shirt.

"Teething?" He wiped the dribble on her chin with the end of her bib.

Caleb nodded. "She's not feeding properly, won't sleep and doesn't even want Wolfie." He lifted Mia's old cuddly toy from the sofa and offered it to Sophie, only for her to start wailing again.

If Rory could've taken the pain away he would have. He hated seeing his niece in pain, and he wasn't used to Caleb being so frazzled either.

"Just let her play with your taser gun or something, Ro." Obliviously knackered, he fell back into a chair still clutching the black and white wolf toy.

"If Mia hears you talking like that she'll taser your arse, mate. Listen, I'll take the girls out for a drive so you can have forty winks. But you owe me big style." With Sophie in one arm, Rory used the other to chuck her things into her bubble-gum pink changing bag.

Caleb looked brighter at the prospect of some peace and quiet. "You know, sometimes this knight in shining armour routine you have going has its advantages."

Between them, they got the girls into their coats. It took a while longer to install the car seats into the back of Rory's car, but soon they were on their way. Where they were going he had no clue, but he could see a relieved Caleb waving them off in the rear-view mirror.

For the Alpha of the pack, Rory was too much of a pushover where his loved ones were involved. One of these days he'd prove he was more than a convenience.

Chapter Four

The smooth movement of the car on the road and the rhythmic swish of the window wipers settled Sophie's cries into a mere grizzle in the back seat. Emily sat contentedly with her colouring books and crayons. Rory quite enjoyed spending time with his niece, and Emily was no trouble. Up until recently he would've said there was a small part of him that liked to be needed.

Since Naomi had let him down not so gently, he simply felt used. He'd given his love and time only to receive nothing in return. As much as he loved his family, he was starting to think he had the shitty end of the stick in all areas of his personal life.

"Poo-ee!" Emily wafted her book around Sophie's car seat. "I think she's got a stinky bum."

The car gradually filled with the unmistakable stench of dirty nappy. *This day just gets better and better.*

The Hills weren't exactly choc full of amenities where he could change a baby, and he was miles from home.

"Shit!" He hit the steering wheel with the flat of his hand.

"Shit!" Emily parroted from the back seat. "Shit. Shit. Shit."

"Er, Emily, that's grown up language. Little girls shouldn't say that word. Okay?" *Fuck!* Naomi would rip him a new arsehole if her daughter took that gem home in her vocabulary.

"Okay, Rory. I won't say shit anymore." She smiled sweetly at him in the mirror.

"Please don't, sweetheart. I'm already in a lot of trouble with your mum as it is." He really didn't need to supply her with any further ammunition to hate him when she already had a full arsenal.

The combination of babysitting stress and the car slowly filling with noxious gases started to make his head hurt. Work would've probably provided a more relaxing environment for his day off. *Work!*

He swung the car around to the sound of Emily 'Whee'-ing in the back like she was on one of those spinning tea cup rides she loved at the fun fair. The one that came once a year. It struck him how sheltered the child's life was out here. Naomi doted on her daughter, but there was so much she was missing out on. If he dared interfere any more than he already had, one of these days he would find out what Ms Duffy was so afraid of out in the big bad world.

In the meantime he'd simply have to entertain Emily the best he could. The pub was out of the question, and, apart from his house, the station was his only option.

Unlike the fortress like battlements of their city headquarters, the Olcan Hills station looked like any other white washed cottage. He pulled up outside as Sophie built up into another wail.

"Okay. Okay. I'll get you sorted out now, sweetheart." A dab hand at the baby juggling now, he managed to get both girls and the changing bag out of the car without breaking a sweat.

He strode into the station with the same confidence he did in his uniform, regardless of his girly accessories. This was his patch after all.

"Hi, Juliette."

"Er, hi, Rory. I didn't expect to see you today." That welcome flush of pink coloured her cheeks.

"I thought I would pop in and say hello. Can you keep an eye on Emily for a minute while I go change Sophie?" It would be easy to offload both girls onto her and do a runner, but Rory always stepped up to his responsibilities. Perhaps that was his problem.

"Sure." She beamed at Emily, then at him. There was no denying how pretty Juliette looked, pale and delicate like a porcelain doll. To have someone gaze at him with such admiration would've been enough for any man to take advantage of the situation. Maybe it was time to move on.

Sophie fidgeted in his arms, reminding him of the actual reason he'd stopped by. "All right, missus. Let's get you cleaned up."

With Emily safely installed beside Juliette in the control room, Rory took the baby through to the waiting room. There wasn't enough room in the bathroom to lay out a clean nappy, never mind a wriggly infant.

He whipped the small changing mat from the bag and unfolded it on top of the leatherette, wipe clean, settee. With some degree of difficulty as Sophie roly-polyed around, he managed to change her.

"Could you keep an eye on this one too for me, so I can go wash my hands?" It was a redundant question as Juliette seemed in her element with the girls. Rory supposed she didn't have much company during the day, save for the odd neighbour calling in to complain about barking dogs or joy riders.

Sophie went willingly to Juliette, fascinated by the silver cross dangling on a chain around her neck. Rory nipped off to the bathroom and back again praying she hadn't noticed he'd gone.

"Thanks for this, Juliette. You're a natural with these two. Maybe I should bring them here more often." How much difference would it make to have someone to turn to when he was the one in need?

"Maybe you should." The look she shot him over the top of Sophie's head left him in no doubt it was more than time with him she really wanted. Shy Juliette was flirting with him and he had no idea what the hell to do about it.

"I suppose I should really check in with their parents first before I offer a day in their esteemed company." It sounded like he was backtracking, but really, he couldn't be sure how thrilled either mother would be to find out he was using their daughters to pick up women.

"I'm sure their parents are grateful for your help. You'll make a wonderful father someday." As she stood with a baby strapped to her hip and holding Emily with one hand, it caused another flutter to Rory's equilibrium.

Standing here, they looked for all the world like a family. For the first time, Rory ached for a scene like this waiting for him at home. The walls of the cottage seemed to close in. Pressure squeezed his lungs and weighed heavily on his heart. Family or career? The time was fast approaching when he would have to pursue one or both instead of remaining stagnant.

"You know you can come see me anytime," she said under lowered lashes.

"Sure I see you nearly every day anyway." He hoped his goofy grin would save him from having to make any promises.

She rolled her eyes but didn't make any further attempt to reprise her Marlene Dietrich impression.

"Okay then. Let's get you two back home before there's another nuclear fallout in Sophie's nappy. Thanks again, Juliette." They did the smalls handover. Rory was so used to doing the exchange with his sister he instinctively kissed Juliette on the cheek.

Her soft skin smelt of soap and flowers, completely different to the exotic spice of Naomi's perfume. Their scents defined their personalities. Where Naomi was powerful, exciting, and intoxicating, Juliette's perfume said safe and comforting. Perhaps a homely girl was what he needed instead of the secretive complicated woman he couldn't seem to stay away from.

* * * *

By the time they got back to Caleb's, the only sound was the soft snoring from the sleeping babes. With his good deed done for the day, Rory vowed to treat himself to a beer as soon as he got home.

Naomi swooped on the car before he'd even pulled on the handbrake. She barely gave him enough time to get out of the driver's seat before she was tugging on his shirt and pulling him away from the girls' hearing.

"Where the fuck have you been?" The ferocity of her tone and language slapped him in the face.

"Caleb was knackered, so I took the girls for a drive. What's your problem?" Immediately on the defensive, he folded his arms across his chest and waited for whatever new barrage of abuse she'd saved for him.

"What's my problem? I came home to find out my daughter was missing and no one could tell me where the hell you'd taken her." Her eyes blazed with a fire Rory envied. If only she could express the same passion for him. It appeared the only time he got her blood pumping was when he'd screwed up again. Which seemed to be happening frequently these days.

Rory was used to Naomi's style of helicopter parenting, hovering around her daughter in case she came to harm. But this was a full on air assault directed entirely at him.

"This is what I get for doing a favour?" He shrugged as he caught sight of Mia and Caleb at the front door. "Caleb was dead on his feet. Sophie was screaming the place down around Emily. You would've preferred I walked away and left them all to it?"

"I would have preferred you did me the courtesy of telling me where you'd taken my daughter." With the message passed on about how pissed off she was with him, Naomi went to wake Emily.

Rory couldn't believe the flak he was taking for trying to help out. Talk about overreacting. "Put it this way, love. It's not the first time I've minded your daughter. I'm not some stranger who'd snatched her off the street."

Naomi unclipped Emily and turned back to face him. "First off, I'm not your 'love'. Secondly, at no point have I ever asked you to help me. Anyway, what the hell was I supposed to think when you wouldn't even answer your phone? You could've been in an accident for all I knew."

Rory patted his pockets in vain. In all the kerfuffle of the afternoon he hadn't even noticed he'd lost it.

A sheepish Caleb stepped into the fray to hand over his mobile. "Sorry, mate. You must've dropped it down the side of the sofa earlier."

"Cheers." Rory took it and shot him a look that hopefully said 'You've dropped me right in the shit here'.

Mia joined them in the driveway and liberated her own sleeping babe. "See, Naomi. I told you there was no reason to worry. Uncle Rory had it covered. Thanks, bro."

The one happy mother restored some of Rory's feel good factor.

"Yeah, thanks. I managed to get a kip and it looks like Little Miss Cranky Pants did too. Hopefully we'll all be back to our fun loving selves soon." Caleb pressed a kiss into Sophie's curls. Apparently absence really did make the heart grow fonder.

If Caleb and Mia thought backing him up would lessen Naomi's wrath, they were sadly mistaken.

"Yes, well. It's different for you, you're family. There's a reason I don't let just anyone take my daughter and I wish you'd respect that." Rant over, Naomi transferred Emily into the Mini and took off, leaving Rory stunned.

He'd be grateful to anyone who could tell him what that reason was so he could stop screwing up.

"Are they still there?" Caleb drew his attention back from the blue blur disappearing down the hill.

"Are what still there?"

"Your balls. I thought she might have chewed them right off."

"You're a funny guy, Caleb Jackson. You see if I ever do you another favour." Even if he wasn't feeling it, he could see the humour in the situation—a burly policeman cut down to size by the pocket-rocket landlady.

"Aww. Don't be like that. You heard what she said. You're family, future bro." If Rory didn't like his sister's partner so much he might've taken out his frustration with a dig in the face.

Instead, he turned to Mia for answers. "What the fuck was all that about anyway?"

"I have no idea. We had a lovely day shopping then all of a sudden she wanted to get home. When Caleb said you'd taken Emily out and we couldn't get hold of you she went ape shit." Mia appeared as much in the dark over her friend's freak out as he. He understood a mother's instinct to protect her offspring, but Naomi bordered on the obsessive. Obviously there was more going on with her than he knew about.

"Well, sis. You know I'm always here if you need me, but I think Rory's Daycare will be shutting up shop for the foreseeable future under fear of death." All his good intentions got him was an ear bashing and a harsh reminder Naomi didn't want him.

Once Mia and Caleb thanked him and apologised again, they went back inside. Rory got into his car with a sigh. He couldn't do right for doing wrong, but there was one person who appreciated him.

He pulled out his phone and scrolled through his contacts until he came to the one he wanted.

"Hi, Juliette. It's Rory."

Chapter Five

They didn't understand. How could they? Naomi doubted any of them lived with the constant fear of being locked away for months—or worse—the way she did. Even after the false alarm, she couldn't settle, her thoughts lingering on what could've happened if those bastards had got hold of her daughter.

She wouldn't apologise for going off at Rory, he knew how protective she was of Emily, if not why. Besides, he was big enough to get over a tongue lashing. And, if it put another sliver of distance between them, all the better. Saturday had only reinforced her belief that she couldn't afford to make attachments. One slip up and her last link to Kian could be gone forever.

As per their Monday morning routine, Naomi left the car at the back of the pub and walked Emily to The Cub Club, clutching her hand tighter than usual.

"Mummy, can I stay at Sophie's house tonight?" Emily looked up at her, eyes filled with hope. She'd become so attached to the baby sometimes Naomi regretted that she would probably remain an only child.

"No, sweetheart. I'm sorry. Sure you'll see all your friends at nursery in a minute." She hated to disappoint her when she asked so little.

Emily scuffed her patent black leather shoes on the kerb as they walked to the traffic lights to cross the road. "It's not fair."

The child was bound to be bored. They'd spent all day Sunday locked away at home with Naomi's increased paranoia. At least she could be sure they were safe there, even if she couldn't quite shake that feeling of being watched.

"Maybe you and me could have a girly night, order pizza and watch a DVD instead."

"Can we paint our nails too?" Emily stopped staring at her toes, much to Naomi's relief.

"Sure. We'll put our onesies on and get really cosy." As the beeping signalled it was safe to cross, Emily practically skipped over the road.

Someday Naomi would have to explain why she couldn't take part in something as simple as a sleepover, but for now, while she could still be easily distracted, Naomi would fudge her way through.

Mia buzzed them into the nursery. "Well, hello, Princess Emily."

She took her little pink rucksack and hung it on the peg below her name. "Can I go play now?"

"Yes, darlin'. Go on in." Mia opened the door to the main playroom where the other kids were already diving into the toy boxes head first. It was always busy in here as shifter kids came from far and wide to be with their own kind.

"I'd better get to work." Naomi wanted to avoid having to explain her outburst on Saturday.

"Is everything all right, Naomi?" She should've known Mia wasn't one to sweep it under the carpet and pretend it never happened.

Even though she had a hand on the door knob, Naomi wouldn't escape without at least acknowledging something had occurred. "It's fine. Emily's my only family. It's only natural that I would react badly to someone taking her without letting me know."

That wasn't strictly true. She had family, somewhere in Donegal. Family who didn't want to know her, and were clueless about Emily.

"Rory was only trying to help. Deep down you know that. I can tell there's something else on your mind. I just wish you would trust me enough to share with me. In the meantime, I'm sure my brother will happily bear the brunt of your frustration."

Naomi winced. Rory had got a raw deal from her lately. Whether he could see it or not, it was for his own benefit. He needed to back the hell off before he got dragged into her nightmare.

"Trust me, Mia, it's nothing you can help me with." Naomi opened the door and stepped out into another dismal day reflecting her grey mood.

She had many friends in the Hills, but when it came to it she was on her own. No one could save her when the hounds came.

* * * *

Unlike most people, Naomi enjoyed winter. It suited her very well when the snow fell and virtually cut Olcan Hills off from the outside world. Although they weren't out of autumn yet, there was a nip in the air that sent punters to The Wild Dog in search of a seat beside the open fire and a bellyful of comfort food.

She made a pot of tea and fetched two bowls of beef stew for the couple patiently waiting in the corner. When it was busy like this it left little time for her to worry.

A draught of icy air blasted the back of her neck. She turned around to see Rory come through the doors with Caleb. They were obviously in a jovial mood, laughing and slapping each other on the back, but as Rory's eyes met hers she saw him tense.

Guilt stabbed her in the heart as those puppy eyes that once looked at her with admiration now held a hint of wariness. No wonder. He was probably waiting in case he said or did something to set her off again.

Nothing in this whole fucked up mess she called her life was his fault, so she did what she did best and pretended all was well.

"Hey guys. What can I get you?" She held her friendly barmaid smile in place until Rory's frown evened out.

"We aren't stopping." Rory still sounded pissed off and she wondered why he'd bothered coming in at all.

"I'm just here for my wages and then I'm off to break bread with my future in-laws." Caleb explained their sudden and brief appearance. His relations with the Blakes had much improved since the birth of little Sophie and Naomi imagined he'd enjoy the meet more than he let on.

"You're all going out for dinner tonight?" Naomi opened the till and counted out the notes as they talked.

"Not me. I have, er, other plans." She could've sworn Rory blushed.

It was so unlike him not to be involved in a family gathering. Or to be so cagey. Despite her attempt at indifference, her curiosity piqued, verging on all out jealousy. Whatever his plans included, they obviously weren't any of her business.

"What brings you here then?" A piece of her inner snark slipped out.

"I wanted to apologise for stressing you out at the weekend. That honestly wasn't my intention." She believed him. Rory would never intentionally cause anyone pain, and really it shouldn't have been him doing the grovelling.

"No harm done." The best she could manage for now as they smiled awkwardly at one another.

Caleb stuffed the cash in his wallet. You want me to play this Friday night again?"

"Yeah. We got a good crowd in last week." Caleb's mix of classic soft rock and popular Irish folk songs certainly kept everyone happy. It took a lot to entice the locals from the outlying farms to stop for more than a pint at night, and she was sure there was more than one illegal poteen still hidden in the hills costing her sales. To have a talent like Caleb who could get people to put their money behind the bar was a godsend.

"In that case I will book you into my busy schedule." Between the baby and renting his land out for grazing to local farmers, he had his hands full.

Naomi thought there was more to these gigs than cash for him. It was his way of cutting loose, and, when Mia could arrange babysitters, she certainly enjoyed watching him here.

A sigh of self-pity almost escaped her. She didn't have a partner to support and love her the way Caleb did. That was entirely her own fault.

"Listen, guys. I have to get on and sort the stock before the evening shift comes on. Enjoy your night. Whatever you're doing."

"See you later, Naomi." Caleb waved as he left. Rory simply afforded her a curt nod.

Suddenly she couldn't wait to pick Emily up from nursery and have someone to hug.

* * * *

As the customers tailed off in the early evening, Naomi found herself clock watching. Business would pick up again after she was long gone. For now she busied herself in the cold cellar, rearranging crates and mentally ticking off her list of things to do before she quit for the night.

The barrels were changed, glasses washed, next week's rota made out, and she'd written instructions out for what she wanted done in the bar tonight. When her fingers were so cold she could barely feel them, she gave up and headed back to the main bar.

"Hi, Marie." The sight of her night manager managed to warm her. She could hand over her responsibilities and head home with a clear conscience.

"Hey, Naomi. How's things?" The busty blonde stepped into the alcove behind the bar to hang her coat.

"All quiet. Thanks for covering the weekend by the way." For Naomi, Marie was the next best thing to having a partner, always there to jump in at a moment's notice.

"No problem. You know I'm happy to do the extra hours." Marie never turned down overtime. Naomi didn't know much about her home life and she didn't ask in case she was expected to reciprocate that sort of information. Like everyone these days, she apparently needed every penny she could get.

"Well, hopefully things will get back to normal this week." Naomi could only hope.

"I don't mean to pry, but is it anything to do with that fella who was here looking for you last night?"

"What fella?" Ice formed in Naomi's veins.

"Tall, dark and yummy. He was asking an awful lot of questions about you. Have you got a secret admirer you're keeping from me?"

"What kind of questions?" Naomi had an irrational urge to slap the grin off her well-intentioned employee's face.

"Oh, you know. When you'd be in again. Where you lived." Marie casually tied her apron around her waist when Naomi was tempted to throttle her with it to squeeze the information out of her faster.

"And you told him?"

"Yeah. He seemed like a nice enough guy and I figured you could do with a dip in the man pool. I'm surprised he didn't call in and see you. Ah well, maybe he'll call by your place."

Yeah, he might swing by with the rest of the pack, murder me, kidnap my daughter...but sure that's the chance you take if you date, right? Fuckety fuck!

"Marie, do me a favour. Don't do me any more favours!" Naomi grabbed her belongings and belted down the street, pulling on her coat as she went.

What the fuck am I gonna do? Panic mode set in. They knew where she was, where she lived. It wouldn't be long now. *What if they're already waiting for me?* It was already dark, the streets deserted, a perfect night for them to strike. She quickened her pace, listening, expecting to hear footsteps behind her.

She blattered on the nursery door, convinced someone would jump her now she'd stopped moving.

"Hold your horses. I'm coming," Mia called from inside.

Why did everyone else seem to be moving in slow motion? Naomi resisted banging her fist on the glass again, and yelled instead. "It's me. I need to get Emily."

Give me my fucking daughter, now!

"She's here. Where's the fire?" Mia unlocked the door with much less urgency than Naomi would've liked.

Fire? She hadn't thought of fire. What if they tried to burn her out?

"Come on, sweetheart. We have to go." Naomi ignored Mia and grabbed her daughter's waist with one hand, her coat and rucksack in the other.

"Is there something wrong, Naomi?" Mia stepped into her path, arms folded as though she was refusing permission for her to go anywhere.

"It's been a long day. I'm tired. I just want to take my daughter home. Okay?" After all these years she still couldn't get used to people wanting to get involved in her personal business.

Mia frowned. "I'm here if you need me."

Tears burnt Naomi's eyes. She'd been strong for such a long time, she hoped she could hold it together now when Emily needed her the most.

She swallowed hard. "Unless you've got a stack of junk food at hand, I think we'll manage. On our own."

Although she didn't look convinced, Mia stepped aside. "I'll see you tomorrow, Em."

"Night, night, Mia." Emily's innocence broke Naomi's heart as she blew kisses. Christ knew what would happen to her if those bastards got their hands on her.

Over my dead body.

Naomi tried to focus on what was best for the moment. Get to the car. Make a pit stop at the house for clothes and money. And worry about everything else once they were on the road.

"Mummy, what's wrong?" Emily struggled to keep up with her along the main street.

"Sorry, sweetheart. We need to get home before we catch cold out here." She did something she hadn't done in a long time and lifted Emily up. They'd save time if she carried her to the car, and having Emily snuggled around her neck brought Naomi some comfort.

Instead of stopping at the pub to say goodbye as she usually did, she had Emily strapped in and the car on the road in record time. Tonight, her fear justified her inability to stick to the speed limit.

Her rented cottage was remote, hidden from the main road by trees. Perfect for someone who didn't want to be found, but it also meant she couldn't see it either until she'd made the drive up the lane.

Fingers of dread tapped her on the shoulder when she spotted an unfamiliar car parked at the side of the house. A dark figure sat inside waiting.

Naomi slammed on the brakes and sent the wheels spinning and mud flying as she reversed at full speed. They weren't taking her without a fight and there was only one person she could turn to for help.

Chapter Six

Rory stepped out of the shower and wrapped a towel around his waist, having washed away all his stresses. The smiling reflection staring at him in the mirror told him he'd made some progress. He'd come to terms with Naomi's rejection after she'd made her feelings very clear by blowing up at him at every given opportunity. And the fact that he actually had a date might have had some effect on his mood too.

He sprayed himself with deodorant and splashed aftershave on his recently shaved face. Although he didn't have any expectations of beginning some epic romance with Juliette, the thought of stepping out into the dating world made him a tad giddy.

She was a lovely girl who did wonders for his self-esteem and he looked forward to spending an evening in her company away from work. The table booked for dinner at a restaurant along the Coast Road meant a bit of a drive, but he didn't think she'd complain when they'd have the sound of the sea lapping on the shore to accompany them on their journey.

A selection of freshly ironed shirts lay on his bed ready for him to choose from, along with clean underwear and his best black dress trousers. He shook his head and laughed, doubting a teenage girl on her first date would be more worried about her appearance than he was tonight.

A hammering on the front door interrupted his impromptu fashion show.

"I'm coming," he yelled, and dropped his towel to pull on his trousers and boxers to preserve his modesty.

No doubt it was Caleb looking for some advice before spending the night with his folks. He made his way to the door, barefoot and bare chested, water dripping from his just washed hair down his torso. If his clothes got any water marks on them he'd kill Caleb. Another pounding rattled the door in its frame.

"For fuck's sake! Hold on!" Whatever his problem was, Rory didn't imagine it warranted criminal damage against his property.

In an equal fit of temper, he wrenched the door open. "Naomi? What the hell—?"

To see her standing on his doorstep, shaking, eyes wet with tears and bottom lip trembling, would have cracked the hardest of hearts. Adding a sleeping Emily in her arms completely melted his.

"I didn't know where else to turn. I can't go home. We've no money, no clothes..." Her rambling didn't disturb him as much as the fear screaming from her every pore.

"Slow down and tell me what's going on."

She looked over her shoulder, automatically giving him the impression of someone being followed. "Can we come in?"

"Sure." He opened the door wide and let them inside, checking the surroundings himself to make sure no one was lurking outside.

"Thank you," she said much too quietly, her head bowed.

Regardless of all that had happened between them he wanted to hug her. He wouldn't of course. Not unless she wanted him to.

"I'm so sorry. I forgot you were going out." She spoke directly to his bare chest.

Shit! Juliette. She would understand if he postponed, wouldn't she? He couldn't leave Naomi in this state.

"No worries. It wasn't anything important. I'll just go and make a quick phone call. And, er, put a shirt on."

"Okay." For the first time in ages she didn't argue with him, simply took Emily into the living room.

Rory stared at the clothes on his bed without really seeing them, his mind and heart being torn in two different directions. It bothered him to have to let Juliette down, but the very fact that Naomi was here, asking for help meant she was in serious trouble.

He could always arrange another date with Juliette. If he turned Naomi away now he might never see her again.

Naomi couldn't stop shaking as shock finally set in. Even though her arms were tired she was loathe to let go of Emily.

Rory returned as she adjusted her position and tried to revive her dead limb. "All doors and windows are locked and bolted. You can put her down now."

The child needed her sleep, but at this point in time Naomi didn't want to let her out of her sight.

"She'll be fine in the spare room. We'll leave the door open so we can hear her," Rory coaxed.

With some reluctance, Naomi carried her precious cargo into the bedroom and tucked her under the covers. Rory watched from the doorway. "Now come into the living room and tell me what's happening."

Under the circumstances, sharing her past was the least she could do. Yet, there were so many parts of that life she didn't wish to revisit with anyone. As she took a seat opposite Rory for the first time since she'd gone on high alert, her thoughts drifted from the imminent danger. It didn't escape her notice he'd covered the slab of solid chest which had greeted her at the door with a plain black shirt.

"I'm guessing for someone who was sick of my interference to turn up here, you're in some sort of trouble?"

Naomi fidgeted with the locket on the chain around her neck, subconsciously reaching for the picture of Kian hidden inside. Where to start? "You've never asked me about Emily's father."

"I wasn't sure I was allowed to." Rory's lopsided grin chipped away another chunk of the burden resting on her shoulders.

"I'll admit I'm not the easiest person to get to know." With good reason. "My life before Olcan Hills is...complicated, to say the least." And now it had come back to haunt her.

"Would a drink help you to share your deep, dark secret?" Even before she nodded, he'd got to his feet and headed down the hall to the kitchen.

A drink sounded like a good idea. Despite owning the pub, Naomi didn't often indulge. She liked to keep her wits about her. Now, with Rory here to protect her it took the pressure off enough to have one drink and kick back, forget about what was out there waiting for her.

"Is white okay?" He handed her a glass of wine.

"Yes, thanks." She preferred it to the bottle of beer he had in his other hand.

"So, Emily's father?" He didn't waste time on meaningless chit chat and got straight to the point.

In some ways it would be a relief to finally share with someone, but not without some liquid courage. She took a gulp from her glass and grimaced at the strong taste. 'Once upon a time' didn't really fit in with the theme of her story. It was no fairy tale.

"My husband, Kian…" She paused for a *what the fuck?* moment, but the unshockable Rory simply raised a dark eyebrow and let her continue. "Yes, I was married. Happily, I might add. Even though my family didn't approve. The O'Connells didn't have a good reputation where we lived, but Kian wasn't like the rest of his family. He was sweet and kind and I loved him very much."

She wound her locket on its chain, seeing the picture of him in her mind's eye—his blond hair falling over his face in that carefree manner she loved.

"Where is he now?" Rory spoke softly, pulling her back to the here and now.

"He died. Before Emily was born." The unexpected catch in her voice proved she still hadn't quite come to terms with the loss after all this time. She swallowed her emotions down with another sip of wine.

"I'm sorry, Naomi." Rory reached over to put a hand on her knee.

"Thanks." To have someone to confide in, to lean on, meant so much, and she'd nearly thrown it all away.

"And your husband's family?"

Naomi knew the time had come to face her demons once and for all. She drained her glass and set it on the coffee table.

"They're bad news. They made our lives hell, making demands and causing problems. When Kian died they tried to...control me. I didn't want that sort of existence for me or Emily." She chose her words carefully, her long standing defences stopping her from sharing all the gory details.

There was no proof they were behind the hit and run that killed her husband. She only knew the O'Connells weren't happy at their plans to leave Donegal with their unborn child. And when she'd discovered what they had planned for Emily she'd known they were capable of anything. Naomi couldn't bring herself to tell Rory what they had done to her after his death. It would destroy her to have him looking at her with pity.

"Is that who you're running from?" His eyes held a steely determination to find out what was going on.

She nodded. "That's why I was so angry about the newspaper article. I've tried to keep Emily safe from them."

"And I ballsed it up." The comfort of Rory's hand on her skin left her as he sat back in his chair frowning.

"You didn't know. But now someone's here, looking for us. There's a car at my house." Nervous tension began to build and she clasped and unclasped her hands.

"I should go over and check it out." He rose, making her panic bubble over.

"You can't! You don't know what these people are capable of. What if they follow you and find us? They can't have her, Rory. They can't." Years of worry caught up with her as she wept. Once she started she thought she'd never stop.

She couldn't see Rory clearly through her veil of tears, but she felt the dip as he sat next to her. He bundled her into a hug that should have triggered her claustrophobia, but in the cage of his arms, against the wall of his chest, for once she was safe.

* * * *

"Oof!" A dig in the ribs ripped Rory from his slumber.

In her sleep, Naomi groaned and thrashed, clearly distressed. The day had taken its toll on her, and once the sobbing had subsided she'd drifted back to sleep. Unfortunately the position they had fallen asleep in had left him with a dead arm and an aching neck.

"Naomi?" He tried to ease his arm out from under her.

"Hmm?" She snuggled in closer to his chest, easing the pressure on his arm.

"Do you want to lie down on the bed?" He flexed his fingers working out the pins and needles.

"Mmm, mmm." There was no effort to move.

Taking matters into his own hands, he scooped her up and carried her to the bedroom. As he lay her down on the quilt, she whimpered and refused to let him leave. What else could he do but stretch out next to her and rock her to sleep?

Only sleep didn't come easy for her. Her brow knitted into a frown as another whimper escaped from her lips. Whatever was going on in her dreams was far from pleasant. He looked on helplessly as she tossed and turned, sweat breaking on her forehead and sticking her dark curls to her pale skin.

"No...please...don't!"

"Naomi? Wake up, sweetheart." Desperate to put an end to her night terrors, he brushed her hair from her face.

A sob sounded in her throat and broke his heart. Obviously she still had secrets that wouldn't stay locked away forever. Why couldn't she trust him more?

"Let me out...please...let me out!" The body shuddering cries were too much for Rory to stand. Whatever these bastards had done he would make them pay.

"Naomi. Wake up!" This time he shook her. It took a moment for her eyelids to flutter open.

"Rory?" The tear-stained, croaky, disoriented version of Naomi was a far cry from her usual ball-busting self. He didn't like it one bit.

"You were having a bad dream. Everything's okay."

"It's not okay. They won't stop until they take Emily away from me." She buried her head in his crumpled shirt and soaked him in her despair, chilling him to the bone.

He pried her off so he could look into her eyes. "No they won't. They'll have to get past me first."

Chapter Seven

Rory scared her. To have someone on her side also meant putting that person in jeopardy.

"I can't risk you getting hurt." The closest words she'd ever found to telling him how important he was to her.

"I can take care of myself. Don't worry." Brushing her concerns aside, he bent to give her a peck on the cheek.

In her head it was an act of appeasement. However, her heart and her body chose to react entirely inappropriately. The warmth of his lips against her clammy skin raised goosebumps all along her arms. His soft touch, a promise of love and kindness, was something she'd denied herself too long from another man.

She tried to convey her wants with one simple look. Rory paused, his mouth a breath away from hers.

"Everything's going to be all right," he whispered on her lips.

At this moment in time, her sight filled only with Rory, she believed him. It took no more than a tilt of her chin to meet him in a kiss. All her anxiety, each of her problems, dissolved in their passion. The taste of beer and longing on his tongue was intoxicating and she intended to drink her fill.

The memory of their first kiss hadn't been exaggerated after all in those long nights she'd spent replaying it. Once afraid that Rory's touch would make her forget her responsibilities, now she welcomed it.

Naomi reached out to stroke her hand along his face. Now she was sure he was real, she wanted him. She slid her fingers down until she could feel the rapid beat of his heart beneath his shirt. Rory joined in to place a rash of kisses along her chin and on that sensitive part of her neck that made her toes curl.

Fabric tickled her collarbone as he opened the buttons of her blouse. He filled the cup of her bra with his large palm, squeezing and teasing her flesh until her nipples pinged to attention.

With a hunger to match hers, Rory stripped off her clothes to cover her body in hot, wet kisses. She only interrupted him long enough to ensure he got naked right along with her. Fair was fair, she'd waited for a vibrator-filled eternity to see what he kept hidden under his bottle green police uniform.

And lord was he an advert for the PSNI! Given his height, she'd always imagined the muscles to match his build. As he loomed over her, his physique definitely lived up to the hype. His biceps flexed when he braced himself on the bed, his large thighs dwarfing hers. The only thing more impressive than the carved six-pack was the breathtaking erection pointing towards it.

When she eventually drew her gaze back to his face he was grinning at her. "Did you get a good look?"

Caught red handed, she smiled back. "Just checking out the goods."

"And? Do I pass muster?" He cocked his head to one side and waited for her to feed his ego.

"You'll do." Her teasing brought a hearty laugh from him to break some of the intensity in the situation.

"I can't say I have any complaints myself." He dipped his head for a full perusal of her offerings.

Naomi fought off the sudden wave of embarrassment as he studied her naked body. It was a long time since she'd shared herself with a man.

"Then shut up and kiss me." She tugged him back up by the hair, but Rory wouldn't submit to her so easily.

"You want me to kiss you here?" He gave her a fleeting kiss on the lips.

"Or here?" He pressed another into the hollow of her throat.

"Maybe here?" He closed his mouth around her nipple and sucked. Technically it wasn't a kiss but this wasn't the time or place to be pedantic.

"What about here?" The one on her belly tickled and she clenched her inner muscles in response.

"Here?" His voice was husky now. Naomi's mouth went dry as he lowered himself between her legs to bury his face in her pussy.

"Yes," Naomi gasped when his tongue parted her lips. Her insides turned to liquid, as her arousal rushed to meet him.

This man should be available on prescription as stress relief.

She surrendered to every lick, every stroke, taking her deeper into a state of nirvana. When he sucked on her most sensitive nub of flesh she nearly burst at the seams. Wet and ready, she buzzed with sexual energy. Alive with need, she squirmed beneath him, impatient for him to soothe the ache in her loins.

She heard him fumble in the drawers next to the bed, and the tear of foil, before he rolled a condom onto his eager erection. They caught each other's eye to exchange nervous, excited smiles. This was a big step for both of them, even if nothing else came of this other than a physical release after years of skirting the attraction.

As if it was her first time, her pelvic muscles tensed as he lowered himself onto her.

"It's okay," he whispered on a kiss.

She responded with an inner sigh and gradually loosened up. It was just as well, otherwise he would've been in danger of losing the tip of a vital piece of his anatomy to her vice-like grip.

"Relax." Rory's breath on her neck tingled right down to that sweet spot where he was poised and ready.

With her breast cupped in his hand, he flicked his tongue over the pebbled peak. He drew it so slowly into his mouth, she was distracted when he joined their bodies together.

After such a long period of abstinence it took a moment for her to adjust as he filled her. This time her moan was one of pure contentment.

Rory kept his cool even though he wanted to howl the house down. Naomi fitted around him like they were made for each other. She'd given so much to him tonight and he didn't know what had happened for him to deserve it. He'd waited so long for her, he sure as hell wanted to make certain she would never regret a moment.

With agonisingly slow movements, he savoured that all-encompassing heat wrapped around every inch of his dick. She bit down on her bottom lip and denied him the full effect of her moans. Call it an ego trip, but Christ he enjoyed hearing her pleasure. He sucked the worried lip into his mouth to release her cries of passion.

It increased his desire to possess her, give her everything he had in return. He groaned and thrust again in response. Naomi clung to him, her legs locked to his waist as she arched to meet every swell of need. Being with her was all he'd dreamt of and more.

A tilt of her pelvis plunged him deeper inside and past the point of no return. He took her mouth again, joined his tongue with hers in a fiery exchange as their bodies rocked together.

His breath came in short bursts as he worked hard to prolong that final moment of bliss, until he was sure his restraint would see him explode. Naomi raced ahead, riding him faster, panting harder. Her screams filled his ears and she coated him in her slick juices, calling him to climax.

He came hard and fast, never letting go of her hips as he poured into her. Dizzy from the powerful force of his orgasm, Rory face-planted onto the bed.

Naomi giggled next to him. "Are you all right?"

"Uh-huh." He barely had enough energy to take the condom off—never mind turn his head.

She rolled onto her side to face him, giving him an attractive view of her cleavage pushed together and laughed again. God it was good to see her like this. Not the naked part, which was a given, but relaxed, and happy.

"Why have we waited so long to do that?" he finally managed when the room stopped spinning.

Her sigh didn't answer the question and the dark look in her eyes only raised more. "Don't spoil it."

He didn't want to be the one to ruin the moment, so he took her in his arms and waited for sleep to claim them.

* * * *

Tired though he was, Rory's police brain refused to shut down for the night. While Naomi fell quickly to slumber, he couldn't help but wonder what haunted her dreams and why she couldn't go home. Whatever her in-laws' reasons for coming for her and Emily, he was the one responsible for leading them here. He wouldn't let them succeed in their quest.

If he'd been protective of Naomi before, now that he'd made love to her she'd just gained her very own round the clock bodyguard. Not the psycho, controlling boyfriend, he liked to think of himself more as the strong, loving Kevin Costner type from *The Bodyguard* film.

The feel good factor of the past hours began to wear off as the O'Connells lurked on the edge of his perfect moment. He kicked the covers off with restless legs. Tomorrow he could go down the whole investigative route and pull up any files he could find on the bastards. Given the reputation they apparently had, there was probably a shitload of past offences. If he found as much as an unpaid parking fine, he'd have them scooped so fast their dirty paws wouldn't touch the ground. He assumed they were wolf shifters like Naomi, but what if they were merely human scum interested in more than babysitting their wolf cub granddaughter?

Careful not to disturb Naomi, he got out of bed to retrieve his clothes from the floor. Once he'd dressed, he went to check on Emily down the hall. Through the crack in the door he could see her curled up, oblivious to the danger around her. He hoped her dreams were full of everything little girls deserved to make them happy.

He double checked the locks and made sure his gun was loaded. He was taking the fight to the O'Connells.

The lights on his car flicked on and off when he pressed the button on his car keys. The Duffy girls were too far off in the land of nod to notice, but he eased the handbrake off and rolled the car down the hill before he started the engine.

In the sensible policeman versus enraged boyfriend internal duel, *I need to keep my job* stopped him from speeding through the hills like every other boy racer out at this time of night.

As he approached her house, he made sure to turn off the car headlights. Not only did it prevent his presence being detected, it also meant he couldn't see anything except black blobs in the dark until he was on top of the suspect car.

He parked behind it and jumped out, with one hand on his weapon at all times. In the dark interior of the estate car he could make out a shape slumped in the front seat. This fucker apparently had no problems sleeping wherever and whenever.

Rory wrenched the door open, spilling the stalker out onto the gravel. He reached down and grabbed him by the front of his jacket. By the time he was slammed against the side of his own car, shadow man started to come to.

"What the fuck?"

Rory launched his fist into the man's gut, leaving him doubled over. "Who are you, and what the fuck do you want with Naomi?"

Score one for enraged boyfriend.

Chapter Eight

There was a flaw in Rory's punch first, ask questions later plan. The arsehole was too winded to answer him.

"I-I—" the recipient of his gut-busting right hook gasped.

Rory took his hands off him, realising he would have to let him breathe if he wanted answers.

"Spit it out!" His patience was thinner than his mother's lips after one of Caleb's near the knuckle jokes.

The stranger straightened up, almost matching Rory in height if not build. "I'm her brother, Liam."

It was Rory's turn to have the wind knocked out of him.

"She doesn't have any family." He'd certainly never heard her mention any.

"Oh, she does. I assure you." Liam folded his arms across his chest, cockier now he'd put Rory on the back foot.

"As much as I'd love to take your word for that, neither Naomi nor Emily has ever mentioned you."

And Rory certainly wasn't about to lead him straight to them on the strength of his say so.

If these people were as ruthless as he imagined, it wouldn't be beyond one of them to lie straight to his face.

Naomi's still-to-be-confirmed sibling reached into his jacket pocket.

Rory's hand twitched on his gun. "Slowly."

Liam opened the jacket wide so he could see he was just reaching for his wallet from the inside pocket. He pulled out a tattered photograph and handed it over.

"It's kinda hard to see in the dark." Rory didn't appreciate being arsed about. Surely he could do him on some sort of harassment charge and lock him up for the night?

"Hang on." Liam reached back into the car and switched on the interior light, illuminating the picture of two dark haired children laughing.

It was easy to pick out Naomi, the spitting image of her daughter at that age. The lanky streak of piss bore the same dimples, the same mop of curly hair. Unmistakably Naomi's family. On closer inspection the only change in Liam since the photo was taken, was the cropped hair replacing the unruly skater boy look.

"What if she doesn't want to see you?" Rory wouldn't make a move without checking with Naomi first. She obviously had her reasons for keeping her distance from him.

"She will. I have one question though." Liam turned off the light and plunged them back into darkness. "Who the hell is Emily?"

* * * *

"Yeah. Sounds like Liam. Don't worry, Rory, he would've found out sooner or later. That's okay. Bring him over." Naomi ended the call and flopped back down on the bed.

Still foggy from another flashback, she found Rory's news difficult to get her head around. While she'd feared the brutality of the O'Connells finally making her nightmares reality, it was her brother who'd thrown her world into turmoil.

Liam. Her little bro who'd been like her shadow growing up, always by her side. Until she'd needed him most. Driven by her desire for an explanation, an apology, and regardless of the late hour she wanted to see him.

She dressed quickly and checked on Emily. Her stomach was in knots as she paced the house, waiting to come face to face with a reminder of her other life. At least this new diversion would take her mind off what had happened between her and Rory.

As glorious and unexpected as it was, she had no clue where they could go now. For so long she'd concerned herself with the consequences of the O'Connells coming after her, she'd never afforded herself the luxury of thinking about a future. What if now she didn't need to run? Could she settle down with someone who wasn't Kian?

The sound of a key turning in the front door alerted her to Rory's return with her brother in tow. As if preparing for a state visit, Naomi tidied the TV remotes on the table and straightened the cushions on the settee. Ridiculous fussing when it wasn't even her home. Anyway, she hadn't needed Liam's approval when she'd married Kian and she certainly didn't need it now.

With childish petulance, she nudged the remotes off the table and messed the cushions.

"Hello, sis." Liam walked into the room ahead of a sheepish looking Rory.

She didn't blame him for anything. Even if this family reunion didn't end in smooshy hugs or running hand in hand through the forest, Liam being her stalker was preferable to the alternative.

"Liam." It didn't seem right to call him Bro like she used to. Older, taller, thinner, he was more than a stranger to her than Rory and Caleb now.

"I saw your piece in the paper." He filled the silence with information she'd already figured out.

"Why did you come?" There must be more reason behind his sudden reappearance than one wee feature in the local rag.

"Maybe I just fancied getting in touch with my big sis, who so happens to own her own pub." At least that infectious smile of his hadn't changed.

"Well, there's no free beer until you tell me the real reason you've suddenly remembered you have a sister." Nearly eight years without the support of her family couldn't be swept under the carpet with a joke and a smile.

"Ouch!" Liam flinched then shrugged his shoulders. "I guess I deserve that. We deserve that."

"Mummy?" Emily wandered into the living room rubbing her eyes. With her bedhead hair and rumpled clothes, she looked like the ragamuffin O'Connell child Liam had probably imagined when Rory spilled the beans.

"Sorry, sweetie. Did we wake you?" Naomi took her daughter by the hand and brought her farther into the room.

Emily yawned, but she had enough wits about her to realise something was going on. She eyed Liam with suspicion and clutched Naomi's hand tighter. All credit to Liam, he dropped to his haunches so he didn't look quite so intimidating to a four year old.

"So you're Emily? Who I've heard so little about." He threw a glance up at Naomi and failed to make her feel guilty about something beyond her control.

"Emily, this is my brother, Liam. Your uncle."

Emily's once narrowed eyes were now wide and staring. "I have an uncle?"

"Two uncles, and a Granny and a Granda. Who I'm sure will be over the moon to meet you." Liam ruffled Emily's hair.

Naomi wished for that to be true.

"Really?" Emily was awake to the point of bouncing.

Everyone in the room turned to stare at Naomi.

"One step at a time." She frowned at Liam for dumping her in a pool of the smelly brown stuff.

"It's late and I have to work tomorrow. Perhaps we should talk this over some other time." God bless Rory. He always knew when to step in.

"I think that's a good idea. We have a lot of catching up to do. Emily, I promise to tell you all about your family, but you need to get back to bed." She ignored her daughter's pout.

"You can sleep on the couch if you want," Rory generously offered to her estranged brother who he didn't know from Adam.

"No offence, mate, but I don't feel like getting cosy with someone who just gave me a diggin' not twenty minutes ago." The tension between the two men left no doubt Rory had done such a thing.

"Well, if you insist on acting like some sort of peeping Tom, it's gonna happen." It appeared Rory was still on for some sort of fight.

The testosterone in the air was too much to deal with at this time of the night.

"Are you two together? Where's Kian?" The irony of Liam's concern about the state of her marriage wasn't lost on her.

That weight of having to recount it all again threatened to crush her. "Rory, I think I'll just take Emily home. Liam can stay in my spare room for now. We have a lot to catch up on."

It was a terrible responsibility to have to disappoint so many people at once, but where the hell would she start trying to deal with everything?

First things first, she ushered Liam and Emily out to her car. Rory waited for her in the living room.

"I'm really sorry. It's just—"

"I understand." That was the trouble, he always understood. Even when she didn't.

"I have to sort things out with Liam before, you know." Was she running again? Perhaps Liam's arrival gave her an excuse to back out of this thing with Rory before it began.

"I'll wait for you." He wrapped his arms around her waist, pulling her in for a kiss.

The moment his lips covered hers, her body went limp, forcing her to cling to him for comfort. He kissed her like it was their last. An enduring memory of his touch, his taste, in one embrace. There was nowhere else she'd rather be.

Chapter Nine

Naomi slipped Emily's nightdress over her head and tucked her into bed. She would be exhausted tomorrow. "Night, night."

"Can Uncle Liam read me a story?" Emily was half-asleep already, but it didn't stop her trying to capitalise on another potential storyteller.

"Not tonight. Tomorrow. I promise." Naomi kissed her daughter on the forehead and switched the nightlight on at the side of the bed.

"It looks like Miss Emily intends to catch up on four years of playtime with Uncle Liam," Naomi informed him as she walked through to the kitchen to flick the kettle on.

Liam stretched up to the top cupboard for two mugs as though he'd lived here with them all along.

"That's okay. I owe her, and you." He slid her a sideways glance as he poured milk into the cups.

These statements he kept making suggested at long last someone gave a damn about her. Naomi let it sink in. Her brother wanted to make things up with her.

All the heartache and sorrow of her enforced isolation welled up until she knew she was going to blub.

"Oof!" Liam gasped as she threw herself at him. "You missed me then, Nome?"

"Don't call me that." At the use of her childhood nickname, she swatted his chest with the palm of her hand.

"What? Nome?" His chest vibrated with laughter under her hand.

She pushed herself off. The happy reunion abruptly ended by his childhood taunt.

"Okay. I promise not to draw attention to your short arse status ever again by likening you to a garden gnome." He crossed his heart and if he ever did it again he would die.

"It's a well-known fact you only called me that because you couldn't pronounce Naomi right." She stuck her tongue out and handed him his tea. "Can we go inside and sit down? I'm shattered."

They moved into the comfort of the small sitting room. The squashy settee looked particularly inviting to someone who had to open the pub in a few short hours. But she and Liam needed to clear the air before sleep could happen.

"Why don't we start with why your useless husband's disappeared and left you and his child to fend for yourselves?" The intervening years certainly hadn't mellowed his feelings about Kian.

A pity. Under different circumstances they might've been good friends.

"My wonderful husband never knew his daughter. He was killed in a car accident before she was born." On bad days it did feel as though he'd abandoned them.

"If we'd known..." The shake of his head and sagging shoulders weren't a sign of grief for Kian, rather a mourning for time lost with Emily she suspected.

"What? Forgiven me for falling in love? Just because Kian's not in the picture it doesn't mean everything's hunky dory." It was this sort of attitude that had driven her away in the first place.

If only they could've accepted Kian for who he was, not what he was.

"We won't open up old wounds. We'll never agree on the subject. I'm sorry for not staying in touch, though. In my defence I was a teenager, and you know that particular species are too self-absorbed to think about anyone else. I had no idea what you were going through. And Emily...how is she?"

"You've seen for yourself. She's fine. She's well provided for, and a friend of mine looks after her while I'm at work."

"You know very well what I mean." Liam frowned and fixed her in a stare very reminiscent of her father's when she'd refused to give in over Kian.

"I don't know which side she takes after if that's what you're getting at. She hasn't turned yet. Although, she was very sick last year which concerned me." Illness wasn't unusual for your average pre-schooler, but wolf shifters rarely got sick. Whatever virus Emily had carried had almost wiped out Rory and Caleb too. Naomi had no clue what her daughter's future held when she came of age.

"With you as her mum, I'm sure she'll be fine whatever happens. What about the rest of the O'Connell clan?"

"We, er, didn't part on the best of terms." She didn't see the point in giving him any more reason to hate the family. If she could help it, the Duffys and the O'Connells would never cross paths again.

"You're well out of it, sis. Are they giving you any grief? Is that the reason the big lad said hello with his fists?"

She couldn't imagine Rory losing control like that. It sent a shiver down the back of her neck to think he would go to such extremes to protect her. She knew him well enough to understand physical violence wasn't the norm for him. It certainly wouldn't do to have two testosterone fuelled alpha males on the rampage.

"I haven't spoken to them since I moved here and I intend keeping it that way." That much was true even if it didn't begin to cover the ways in which she'd suffered at their hands.

"Mum and dad will be pleased." The olive branch came at the price of her husband.

It didn't change anything as far as she was concerned. "It was their choice to cut me out of their lives. I don't give a monkey's what they think. I never did. I loved Kian, he loved me and he was a good man. His death was a tragedy, not something to crow about."

"Believe me, I don't take any joy in the fact you were widowed so young, or that Emily never knew her father. But it's time to build bridges. You both need your family around you. And I, I need you." Liam reached across to hold her hand. A gesture Naomi was grateful for.

"One step at a time, Liam." These past twenty-four hours had turned her life upside down. She needed space to think before things changed beyond all recognition. For better, or worse.

* * * *

Dread lined Rory's stomach as he started his working day. He sat outside the station in his car, sipping his takeaway coffee in the hope it would fuel him through his shift. He was still drowsy from lack of sleep caused not only by Liam's appearance, but also Naomi's changeable attitude.

One minute she was yelling at him, the next cuddling up to him like she belonged in his arms. After making love to her last night, he didn't think he could cope with another Naomi switcheroo. Not now when he knew she was the only one he'd ever want.

He drained his paper cup. There was no point delaying the inevitable. He would have to face Juliette sometime. Technically he hadn't cheated on her since they'd never gone on a date. So why did he feel like such a cad?

"Hey." He raised a hand in greeting and waited until she ended the call she was on.

"Hey, yourself." Her smile didn't hold the same dazzling wattage as usual.

I'm a shithead.

"I'm really sorry about last night." Sorry he let her down, not sorry he'd finally got together with Naomi. If he'd thought there was a flicker of hope there he would never have arranged the date with Juliette in the first place.

"Don't worry about it." She busied herself with files, not meeting his eye.

He would have preferred she slapped him.

"Something came up. I don't think it would've worked out between us anyway when we have to work together." It was difficult to apologise and backtrack at the same time. He would never have made it as a player. His conscience would never have allowed it.

"No. You're right. Let's just forget it." Her tip-tapping on the computer grew louder and faster as she directed her anger at the keyboard instead of him.

"Juliette—" What more could he do?

The door opened and one of last night's main events walked in. "Naomi said I could find you here. Can we talk, Rory?"

Right now, making conversation with Liam would get him out of this ball-shrinking conversation with his co-worker.

"Absolutely. Juliette, this is Liam, Naomi's brother. He just got into town last night." *See, he's the reason I cancelled. Definitely not because I was having great sex with the love of my life.*

"Hello, Juliette." Liam almost walked through him to get to the receptionist.

"Hi. I hope you're enjoying your stay in the Hills so far." Juliette perked up at the attention as he shook her hand.

"It certainly has its attractions." Liam's sly wink sent Juliette the delightful shade of crimson usually reserved for Rory.

It gave Rory a taste of his own medicine to be blown out for someone else without a second thought.

"Liam? You wanted to talk? Juliette, give me a shout if anything comes in." Rory jangled his keys to let them know he was leaving with or without his newly acquired pain in the arse.

"I'm coming." Liam followed him out without taking his eyes off Juliette.

Rory half expected him to make a sweeping bow as he left, such was the cringy display of Liam's flirting.

"Do you want to go to The Dog?" Rory could do with seeing Naomi and trying to gauge where he stood with her in the cold light of day.

"Nah. We need to go somewhere my sister can't eavesdrop. Is she single?"

"Naomi? I, er, you'd need to ask her." Rory daren't say anything that might incriminate him and may be used against him at a later date.

"No, Juliette. You tool. Naomi told me all about you two last night." Liam looked at the closed station door as if he might make a sudden rush inside again.

"Really? I wish she'd tell me. And, yes, Juliette's single." Did he really want to encourage a match there? It would get him off the hook with Juliette, but he hadn't mentioned the date that never was to Naomi. What if it got back to her?

"Hmm. Right. Where was I? Yes. Naomi. We need to go have that talk." Liam definitely didn't possess the same focus as his sister.

* * * *

Rory chose to take Liam home with him, where no one would hear or interrupt. These days his house was fast becoming a focal point in his social life. Roll on the warmer weather when it gave him more options than merely the Dog and the station.

Liam didn't stand on ceremony and took a seat in the living room. "So, talk. What's the deal with my sister?"

Rory liked his forthright attitude. He didn't have time for pussy-footing around either. "What do you want to know?"

"It's none of my business what's going on between you two. I'm more concerned about the O'Connells. I assume the hit I took was meant for one of them? Does that mean you've had contact?" The scowl on Liam's face reminded him of Naomi's when she'd spoken of her in-laws.

"I know very little about them." A big part of Rory would relish a run in with them so he could see exactly what sort of scum he was dealing with. "Naomi came to me last night scared witless that they were coming to take Emily away. Care to shed some light on why that's the case?"

It had taken years to get her to share as much as she had last night, but it wasn't enough. Whatever had her running scared, he needed to know. So he could put a stop to it once and for all.

"Saying the O'Connells have a bad reputation is akin to saying Hitler was a naughty boy. You name the crime, they've probably committed it. Drugs, fuel laundering, identity fraud, right down to plain theft. Hence, why our parents didn't approve of the match. Naomi insists Kian wasn't like the rest but mud sticks."

She must have really loved Kian to be blinded by his extended family.

"I get it. They're horrendous human beings. But why would they want Naomi and Emily so badly?" Rory didn't see what financial gain or otherwise there could be, unless they wanted a share in the pub.

Liam leant forward in the chair, resting his forearms on his knees. "She hasn't told you then?"

"Told me what?" Rory was getting mighty sick of being kept in the dark.

"The O'Connells—they're not pure breeds like us. They're wolfhounds."

Rory had never come across wolfhound shifters before. Although, it would certainly explain their outcast status. And Naomi's reluctance to share details of Emily's parentage. Legend had it that when wolves were dying out of Ireland, they were bred with hound dogs. A shifter must've been mated somewhere down that line for the anomaly to occur in the shifter community.

"What does that mean for Emily?"

"We don't know yet. Her mother's a wolf shifter, her father a wolfhound. She could turn either way. I imagine that's why the O'Connells would come after her. Rumour has it some of the family have tried to mate forcibly with wolf shifters so they can breed out the hound stigma. A female wolf shifter, even a half breed, would be a valuable commodity to them." Liam didn't need to spell it out. When she was of age, Emily could be used in some sort of breeding programme to reintroduce the wolf gene to the O'Connell line.

"It's no wonder Naomi freaked out when she thought they'd tracked her down."

"If I could do it with no more than a newspaper and a sat nav, I'm sure those mangy mutts can manage it." No doubt feeling as impotent as Rory, Liam scrubbed his hands over his face.

"They'll have to get past me first." After fighting for Naomi for so long, he wouldn't let her, or her daughter, fall into the hands of such hateful bastards.

"And me." Amber flashed in Liam's eyes as his wolf poised, ready to fight.

Pain in the arse or not, Liam at least provided some back-up. If the O'Connells so much as set foot in Olcan Hills, they'd start a shifter war.

Chapter Ten

"You're firing on all cylinders, girl," Mia called across the bar.

Naomi gave her a quick wave and finished serving her customer before she could take time out to speak to her friend. "That's seven pounds sixty eight please."

"I'll have a ham and cheese toastie and a cuppa if you're still serving." An impatient Mia pushed her way through to the counter.

"Lunch time is nearly over, but anything for my favourite Emily minder." Naomi jotted down the order and handed the ticket into the kitchen.

"I thought I would treat myself today and have lunch with people over the age of five." Mia didn't usually come in mid-week. Perhaps she'd heard rumours about the goings on at Rory's, or her new visitor.

Naomi could do with someone to share her news with and get some advice on how to proceed with Rory and Liam.

"Marie, I'm taking my break." Her second in command was putting in some extra hours and Naomi reckoned she was capable of handling the rest of the customers.

She directed Mia to a table in the corner, far enough away from the bar that they wouldn't be disturbed, but still within view of the bar in case she was needed.

"I understand you had a busy night, madam. Your car at Rory's half the night...a mysterious stranger looking for you..." Mia took a sip of the tea Marie brought her and waited for Naomi to fill in the blanks.

"I, um..." *I thought the scumbags who killed my husband had tracked me down, so I took refuge at Rory's, and somehow happened to fall into bed with him. Oh, and then my brother, you know, the family I never told you about, turned up.*

"Just tell me you and my brother finally got it on, and I'll be happy." Mia rushed her to answer.

"Yes, we, er..." Naomi's cheeks burned at discussing such private matters. She couldn't bring herself to say it out loud when such explicit pictures came to mind of Rory on top of her, doing such wondrous things to her body.

Mia held a hand up to stop her. "Judging by the colour of you, and the distant look in your eyes, I'll take that as a yes. Don't worry, I don't expect details. He is my brother after all."

The look of disgust on Mia's face made Naomi laugh out loud. It encouraged her to tease a bit more. "And what a man he is."

"Eww!"

Marie interrupted to bring Mia's lunch but the interrogation didn't stop.

"And who was the hottie asking around after you? You left in such a flap last night I was sure it had to be a jealous ex or something." It was only natural for Mia to assume that was the cause of Naomi's distress when it wasn't that long ago she'd had to deal with her own stalker ex-boyfriend.

Naomi cleared her throat. At some point she would have to fill her friend in on the whole sorry O'Connell saga, but not now when she was still on a high from the night before. Maybe she'd take out a full page ad in the paper so she wouldn't have to keep repeating herself.

"It was Liam, my brother." *Duh, duh, duh.* There really should have been some sort of ominous music playing as she dropped the bombshell.

"Your what?" Mia's eyes nearly popped out of her head, and her toastie hung in mid-air as her mouth dropped open.

"My brother. Yes, I have family, but as you know I haven't spoken to them in years." If last night was anything to go by it wouldn't be long before this snippet of information spread like wildfire through the village too.

Mia set her lunch back down on the plate. "I don't know what to say. I heard some fella dropped Emily off this morning at work, but I never guessed... And how are things now with this brother?"

"Good. I think. I don't know what his immediate plans are, but he stayed with me and Emily last night."

"That must have been nice."

"Weird, but nice." Although she wasn't used to opening up her home to anyone, having Liam there reminded her she wasn't alone in the world.

"Has Rory met him yet?" Mia wolfed down her snack waiting for the next instalment of the Naomi Duffy reality show.

"You could say that." Rory would never live it down if she squealed to Mia that he'd walloped him one.

"I can't wait to meet him, and I'm sure Caleb would enjoy some more male company around here." The not so subtle hint for an introduction mightn't be a bad idea.

"We could all meet up here later for a drink if you want? Oh, but what would we do with the girls?" The immediate threat may have passed, but Naomi wouldn't leave her daughter with just anyone.

"I'll tell you what. I'll phone mum and dad to see if they fancy a spot of babysitting. Ms Duffy going out on the piss is too much of an opportunity to pass up on." Mia left the money for her lunch and scurried back to work before Naomi could object.

As she sent a message to Rory suggesting the meet, Naomi's insides danced a merry jig. This could be construed as their first official date.

* * * *

Naomi's unexpected text lifted Rory's spirits no end. After he'd left Liam and gone back on patrol, his head was full of more questions surrounding Naomi than ever. Her invitation to get together with everyone at the pub seemed like a step in the right direction to answer one of those questions — Did she want anything more than a one night stand with him?

It might only be a drink in the local, but to Rory it signified so much more. Traditionally this was the point where Naomi beat a hasty retreat. He gave himself a smile in the mirror as he shaved. They couldn't get much closer. This night represented a change in their relationship. Hopefully now they had one.

He took his time getting ready, choosing his best shirt and black trousers. A tie proved too much, so he whipped it off again and left the top button of his shirt undone.

* * * *

Naomi and Liam were already standing at the bar with drinks in hand when he arrived.

"Can I get you a beer?" Liam immediately settled the nerves in Rory's stomach.

For some reason he suddenly felt like a bumbling school boy on a first date.

"That would be great. Thanks, Liam." Rory turned to Naomi and his mouth went dry.

Instead of the uniform she always wore to work, she sported a grey knitted dress. It wasn't anything fancy, or remotely revealing. Yet, the way it clung to the curves Rory now knew so well, she may as well have been naked.

"Hi," she said with a hint of shyness.

For the life of him he didn't know what to say. *You look fantastic. Are you coming home with me tonight?*

He settled for, "How're you?"

"I'm great. Your parents have agreed to mind Emily and Sophie for the night so I can let my hair down for once." She held her glass up in a mock toast before she took a sip of wine.

Naomi looked happier, more relaxed than he'd ever seen her. She was beautiful.

"Here you go." Liam passed Rory his pint, stopping him from dropping to his knees to declare his love for the landlady.

"Cheers!" A mouthful of the amber nectar at least wet his lips, even if it couldn't reach the parts he most needed help with.

Rory jammed his hand in his pocket and discreetly adjusted himself so the crotch of his trousers weren't so damn tight.

"Oh, here they are." Naomi directed his attention to the door, where Caleb and Mia made their entrance.

At least with these two he didn't feel under pressure to impress.

"Liam, this is Rory's sister, and my best friend, Mia. And this is Caleb, her husband to be." Naomi made the introductions to handshakes all round.

"Pleased to meet you, Mia. I see you got all the good looks in the family." Liam got the banter off to a start.

Rory followed suit. "It seems Naomi here is what they call a double threat. She got the beauty and the brains in your family."

A chorus of 'Ooh's' sounded. Followed by, "Looks like you've met your match, mate."

Somewhere during the gales of laughter a round of drinks was ordered and they all settled down for a good night in each other's company.

* * * *

In her boozy haze, life looked good to Naomi. With family and friends around her, and the love of a good man, all was rosy in her garden. She stole a peek at Rory across the table. He looked hot tonight. Usually there was nothing did it more for her than his full police uniform, but that shirt was so tight around his biceps, and those trousers left little to the imagination.

Lucky for her she had the real deal perfectly preserved in her wank bank. Not prone to frequent bouts of horniness, she took another glug of wine. Perhaps it was time for her to be selfish for once. People in here were always saying a little of what you fancy did you good when they were knocking back copious amounts of alcohol. Well, there was only one thing she fancied…

"Rory, can I have a word with you?" She blurted out across all other conversations going on around the table.

"What? Now?" His confusion was understandable.

They'd barely spent a moment alone this evening — probably because she didn't want the gossip starting. But now she was actually enjoying herself she didn't want to waste another second worrying about what other people might do.

"Yes. Now." She got to her feet a tad shakily, knocking the table as she excused herself.

Rory nudged out past the others to meet her in the middle of the floor. "What's up?"

"I just wanted to make one thing clear." She focused on him as well as she could under the circumstances.

"What's that?" Rory's adorable frown made her intentions all the easier."This." Naomi threw her arms around his neck and pulled his head down to meet hers.

She kissed him as though there was no one else in the room. For a moment there wasn't. Not to her at least. All she could think about were his arms circling her waist, his lips submitting beneath hers in an unspoken declaration of love. Only the hoots and hollers from the peanut gallery stopped her from going any further.

They broke apart and Rory ducked his head as applause rang out. "I guess that makes us official then?"

"I guess it does." Point well and truly made, she took his hand and headed back to the table.

"About bloody time." Caleb slow clapped them back to their seats.

"Phew! I thought we were going to have to chuck a bucket of water over you two." Mia fanned her face and gave Naomi a wink.

"There are some things a brother shouldn't have to see." Liam gave an exaggerated shudder. Naomi punched him in the arm as she sat down.

Rory kept hold of her hand, squeezing it as if telling her he knew how much it had taken for her to out them as a couple so publicly.

"I'm starting to feel like a gooseberry here," Liam muttered into his pint glass.

Naomi ruffled his hair. "Ach, bro. You're not a total troll. I'm sure you'll bag yourself a date eventually."

"I thought you had your sights set on Juliette over there?" Rory nodded towards a group of women at the bar.

Naomi recognised the young redhead from the police station. Liam worked quickly for someone only in town five minutes.

"I can't simply stumble over there and ask her out like any other sleaze she's ever met in a bar. Where's the romance in that? I need some sort of grand gesture." It appeared Liam had been giving his next move a great deal of thought. Maybe there was more to him than his laddish demeanour would suggest.

It saddened Naomi that she knew virtually nothing about the man he'd become. A situation she hoped to rectify in the near future.

"Why don't you invite her to the wedding?" Mia suggested.

"Good idea. There's nothing that'll get a girl into bed faster than reminding her she's still on the shelf." Sometimes Caleb's humour went too far, but the glazed look in his eye said it had more to do with the beer.

Mia gave her fiancé a shove. "Ignore him. The wedding's a few weeks away, and you're definitely invited. She could be your plus one."

"Thanks. I might take you up on that. So have you guys got everything organised?"

"Venue. Food. Dress. Yeah, I think we're good to go." The permanent smile on Mia's face since she and Caleb had got together made it obvious she'd be content if they did the deed in a Las Vegas drive thru.

"There was one thing we forgot. The stag night. Rory, you let me down mate." Caleb slumped in the corner shaking his head.

"My bad." Rory held up his glass in apology, managing not to look the least bit sorry.

A drunken night in Belfast with Caleb would probably be too much even for a PSNI officer to handle.

"I didn't get my hen night either." Mia pouted.

With only two girls in their 'party' Naomi didn't imagine it would've been a landmark occasion anyway.

"We could count tonight as a joint hen/stag do. We're all here and we've got booze." It seemed logical to Naomi, not to mention economical.

"Hmm. It means I don't get strippers though. I want my strippers!" A petulant Mia demanded her man candy, sending Naomi into fits of giggles.

A suddenly animated Caleb bounced to his feet. He slammed his empty glass on the table making them all jump. "You want strippers, sweetheart? You got strippers."

The group pivoted in their seats and watched him strut over to the alcove where he performed his sets on Friday nights.

"What are you doing?" Rory was the first to query his actions, even if Naomi had a bad idea she knew what was coming next.

"Duh! Stripping! And I expect my best man to get his arse up here beside me." Caleb started to unbuckle his belt.

Naomi wasn't so inclined to stop him now there was potential for her man to show off his goods too.

"No chance!" Much to Naomi's disappointment, Rory wouldn't even entertain the idea.

"I'm up for it." Liam downed the rest of his pint and went to join The Dog's latest stage show.

The general hubbub of the pub died down as all eyes turned to the drunks on parade.

"Are they seriously going to do this? Oh, I have to save this for posterity." Mia pulled out her mobile phone to capture whatever spectacle was about to unfold.

"Rory, come on." Caleb beckoned him over to the brotherhood of drunken arses.

Liam started to chant. "Rory. Rory. Rory."

Soon, the whole bar joined in.

"All right. All right. Obviously you need some beef to go with your cake, boys." Rory took one last gulp of beer. Apparently there was nothing like peer pressure to get a man to abandon his inhibitions.

All Naomi could do was sit back and enjoy the show.

Chapter Eleven

"What? No music?" Rory walked towards them, his arms open wide.

It gave Naomi a warm glow inside to see him so chilled out. It also made her lady parts tingle with the anticipation of his strip. It wouldn't do to have him change his mind now.

"Marie! We need music!" she bellowed before another fit of giggles.

The boys huddled together while Marie chose a suitable tune to strip to. As the seventies boom-chick-a-wah-wah music played, Naomi whooped and clapped along with the rest of the town.

"I never thought I'd see the day when my big brother would get his kit off for a laugh. Actually, I'm not sure I want to. You watch him, I'll keep my eyes on the sexy blond at the end." Mia leaned closer with her camera phone.

"Yes. I think I'll pretend Liam isn't there either and concentrate on the hunk in the middle." Said hunk began to unbutton his shirt and reduce Naomi to a puddle of drool.

It said a lot when the width of his smile distracted her from his pecs. Although, not for long. He ripped his shirt open the rest of the way to reveal a set of abs she thought she'd imagined in last night's excitement.

The cheers grew louder, and with no evidence of team co-ordination the guys stripped off their top halves. Naomi made a grab for Rory's shirt as he tossed it to the baying crowd. She snatched it from the air like a spinster bridesmaid at a bouquet toss. Mia too made her claim on Caleb's T-shirt, and Liam's landed squarely in Juliette's hands.

With some attempt at dance moves, the boys swung their hips left, then right, and whipped their belts from their trousers. Rory even performed a twirl before snapping the leather taut between both hands. Naomi thought she would come there and then.

"I think he's done this before," she sighed.

The belt slithered to the floor, neglected as focus shifted to unzipping his fly. A little shimmy and all three dropped their kecks. Laughs and gasps accompanied the local talent standing in their trunks with their trousers round their ankles. The music played on.

Rory stood with only a pair of black boxer briefs to preserve his modesty. *Would he actually take them off and do the full monty?* She knew Caleb and Liam wouldn't have any qualms about getting their bits out, but she didn't want Rory to regret anything tomorrow. If the evening panned out to her liking, she'd make sure she got a private performance later anyway.

As the music came to a crescendo, the trio did a one-eighty turn and wiggled their arses. Naomi watched from behind her fingertips. The crowd was in a frenzy as all three hooked their thumbs into the waistbands of their underwear.

Caleb started the countdown. "Three. Two. One…"

One by one, her friend, her lover and her brother, pulled down their knickers. And mooned. Three perky white bums shook at the audience, sending them all into hysterics. Naomi and Mia included. They roared until tears ran down their faces.

When the applause rang out, the backsides were promptly covered up again.

"Thank you. Thank you," they mouthed and took a bow, ignoring the cries for more.

Caleb and Rory returned to the table while Liam went in search of his redheaded beauty.

"Hmm, I think I'll take this one home." A lusty Mia greeted Caleb with a sexy smooch.

Naomi didn't fare so well as a sudden attack of modesty hit Rory. "Can I have my shirt back please?"

"Um, no. I think I prefer this look on you." She feasted her eyes on the slab of man meat next to her.

"It's bloody freezing, you know."

"I can see that." His pointy nipples hadn't gone unnoticed.

It took sheer strength of will not to pucker up and suck on them. She was sure their reputation as upright citizens in the community was shot to hell anyway.

Naomi tucked the shirt under her bottom. "If you want it, you'll just have to take it from me."

Rory leaned in until his breath tickled her ear. "Oh, I'm not gonna take it, love. I'll wait until you want to give it to me."

Arousal shot through her so fast, her ovaries were in danger of exploding.

I'll get down on my knees and give it to you now, sexy.

She checked her watch, with a sudden urge to swap their great night out for a fun night in.

* * * *

Goosebumps set up camp on Rory's skin as stubborn as hell Naomi insisted he remain bare chested. He had two reasons to be grateful when they called it a night. The shirt was wrinkled when she reluctantly handed it back.

"I'm sure there must be a law somewhere that says you're required to stay partially naked at all times." Naomi's ego-boost stopped him from worrying that he'd killed his career with one flash of his arse.

"Fortunately there isn't." He shrugged on his shirt and buttoned up his modesty.

Caleb and Liam were definitely a bad influence. He tended to act the eejit right along with them and it wouldn't be long before their wolfie selves were running wild in the woods not caring who saw them.

"Judging by the admiring glances coming your way, I don't think I'm the only one who wishes there was. Maybe I should employ you as one of those naked bar tenders and stick a bowtie on you..." She tapped her finger on her lip and eyed him up as she thought it over.

"Thanks for the compliment, even though I'm starting to feel objectified. That was my first and last count of public indecency. But, if you take me home now, I'll let you stick anything you want on me." He wiggled his eyebrows, in keeping with the fun theme.

The speed with which Naomi finished her drink and got to her feet left him dizzy. "Then what are we waiting for?"

"See you later, guys." Rory may as well have been talking to himself for all the notice Caleb and Mia took, making out like they were already on their honeymoon.

"Where's your car?" Naomi asked as they stepped out into the night.

"I parked it at the back of the pub out of sight. Why? There's no chance either of us are driving home. I'll get it in the morning." In hindsight, perhaps he should've phoned a taxi, or told her earlier she'd have to hoof it back home.

With determined strides in her black heels, which were incredibly sexy now he noticed them, Naomi walked towards the car.

"I think we're okay here." She stopped and looked around.

"Yes, the car's safe. Can we go now? It's pitch black out here." Olcan Hills didn't have a great need for streetlights when the locals had such excellent night vision.

"That's the idea." She walked around to the back of the car and hopped up onto the boot.

"What are you doing?" Clearly, the drinking had sent them all doolally.

"Waiting for you." Mischief glinted in her eyes as she lay back.

"I don't know what they put in the drink around here, but I think I like it." Rory positioned himself between her legs and bent down to kiss her.

With moves worthy of an American wrestler, she wrapped her legs around his waist and pulled him closer. Caught off balance, he fell forward and landed flat out on top of Naomi.

Her dress rode up her thighs to give him a peek of lacy black stocking tops. His cock responded appropriately. "Are you trying to seduce me, Ms Duffy?"

"Is it working?" She shoved her hands down the back of his trousers and grabbed his backside, making it crystal clear what she wanted.

At his hesitation, Naomi renewed the kiss, dipping her tongue into his mouth to create a spark that set him on a one way path. The base nature of his position, his hard-on pressed against the soft mound of her pussy, called directly to the wild side of him already on the prowl tonight.

"Are you sure?" He waited for the green light before he raced out of the trap.

"Have you got any protection?" The first flicker of doubt crossed Naomi's face.

At times like this he was glad he'd been a boy scout. He took time out from their dry humping to pull a condom from his wallet. "With you, I'm always ready."

Naomi snatched the foil packet from his grasp and ripped it open.

"Get 'em off," she ordered before popping the rubber in her 'O' shaped mouth. He couldn't drop his trousers fast enough.

Naomi slipped off the car to crouch before him on the ground. In one slow, exquisite motion, she sheathed him with her mouth. His legs quivered at such an intimate, erotic interaction. When she stood up and assumed her horizontal position back on the boot, she winked.

That did it. He pulled her legs towards him until her arse was on the edge of the car and ripped her panties off. He took hold of his cock and plunged it into her pussy. The sudden coupling gave him instant satisfaction, but he wanted more. He wanted all of her.

He hooked Naomi's knee to lift her leg higher, plunge deeper.

The cold night became a distant memory as her tight heat wrapped around his dick. The raw pleasure of being inside her was only surpassed by pride at her moans of satisfaction. Driven by her escalating cries, Rory thrust into her with zeal. He clenched his buttocks and struck at her core. Who said lightning couldn't hit the same place twice? According to Naomi's cries he'd hit it with astounding accuracy time and time again.

Her obvious enjoyment brought out the savage beast in him and all he wanted to do was claim his mate completely. He buried himself deep inside her, knotting them together so tight he never wanted to let go. Only her wrapping reminded him they were still in their human form. The abrasion of her stockings against his skin as their bodies rubbed together, built up the static charge between them. Until he was at the point where one more brush of lace would send sparks flying.

Naomi arched up off the car, her inner muscles opening and closing around his shaft as her moans grew shriller, maintaining eye contact through every wave of her impending climax. Only when she reached that final swell of ecstasy did she throw her head back and drift away from him. One last cry and she squeezed him into early surrender. They pierced the night with the vocal outpouring of their orgasms.

The panting took a while to subside, as did the rapid beat of Rory's heart as he recovered from his unexpected outdoor workout. Although it had to be said this was preferable to a morning in the gym.

It was too cold, too public, to hang around with their knickers around their ankles. Within minutes they'd redressed and were on the road to Rory's house, arm in arm.

"I guess brewer's droop isn't an infliction you suffer from?" Naomi seemed quite pleased with her spontaneous seductress routine.

"In that outfit you could make cooked spaghetti hard." Rory reached down to give her cute butt a squeeze.

"Is that a challenge?" She reciprocated the squeeze, albeit in his groin area, and thankfully more gently.

"It could be, but I suggest we find out behind closed doors this time. Before we both get us arrested for lewd behaviour." In a sudden burst of energy, Rory scooped Naomi off her feet and carried her back to his cave.

Chapter Twelve

They fell through the door in a tangle of limbs and half removed clothing. Naomi simply couldn't get enough of him tonight. Free from responsibilities and worries she was able to give in to the passion for Rory, too long held in check.

Her mouth never left his as they stumbled towards the bedroom, shedding the rest of their clothes en route. By the time they had made it to the bed, they were naked and wanting.

Rory's breath was hot on her skin as he placed a necklace of kisses around her throat. The feather light brush of his lips teased her with promise. Her body thrummed with the anticipation of him taking possession.

When he reached up to hold her wrists in his large hands, she was abruptly pulled out of the moment and catapulted into the past. Even though Rory's tight grip was fired by lust, and nothing more sinister, Naomi couldn't stem the fear bubbling up inside her. That pressure on her wrists reminded her of the chains biting into her skin, leaving her red raw if she tried to move.

For too long she'd been a victim, powerless in her struggle against captivity. Rory's bedroom melted away to leave her in that small, dark room, hidden from the light and invisible to the world.

"Let me go!" She bucked against him, twisting and turning in his grasp.

Her breathy gasps were no longer a result of building desire, but a genuine need to draw air back in her lungs.

"Are you okay? Did I hurt you?" Rory relinquished his hold immediately and Naomi scrabbled up the bed into a sitting position.

"I don't like the feeling of being pinned down. That's all." She steadied her breathing and rubbed at her wrists. The emotional scars ran deeper than the physical ones ever had.

"You know I would never do anything to hurt you." Rory ran the palm of his hand along her outer thigh.

Unable to turn off her distress at the flick of a switch, she flinched.

"I'm sorry." Tears burned the back of her eyes. *Would she ever be fully free of her demons?*

Rory moved up to sit beside her at the head of the bed and pulled the covers up around them.

"There's nothing to apologise for, Naomi. We'll take things at whatever pace you're comfortable with." His voice was calm, reassuring enough for her to rest her head against his chest.

"It's not that. After all, I set the pace tonight if you recall." She hated that the past insisted on holding her back.

"Whatever it is that's still haunting you, causing you to retreat like an injured animal, you can tell me." He probed without making demands on her.

Naomi hugged her knees and rocked, drawing comfort from her own arms as she did during her worst days. Would it hurt any more than it already did to share her troubles?

"I didn't tell you everything the O'Connells did after Kian died."

"No?" His voice hardened as he shifted beside her.

"They're wolfhound shifters." She waited for a response, but apart from the sound of his teeth grinding together, he remained silent. "Kian's father has wanted the O'Connell line to be bred back to pure wolf shifter for a long time. When Kian and I married, it was for love. Neither of us gave much thought to the consequences."

She watched Rory's expression darken with murderous rage. "Did they hurt you?"

When she didn't answer immediately, he took hold of her chin and turned her face to his. "Did they hurt you?"

His brown eyes shimmered with angry tears—a sight which warmed and saddened her.

"Not in the way you think. I was already carrying one of the crossbreeds they'd hoped for. Once Kian died they needed to make sure the child would remain under their control. I'm not convinced they didn't have something to do with his death since they went to such effort to make sure I couldn't leave."

"What did they do to you?" His frown deepened with every second she delayed telling him.

"They kept me chained in the attic like some sort of dirty family secret. I was kept in complete lockdown so even if I had the energy to shift, there was no means of escape." The cramped conditions and lack of exercise, not to mention the worry for her unborn baby, meant she hadn't dared to shift again after her initial attempts to run.

"For how long?"

"Weeks. A month maybe." The days after Kian's funeral were a blur. "I was just an incubator for their redemption. They only wanted the baby. Whatever sex it was, it would inherit my wolf genes or be a cross of our two shifter identities. They thought it was the key to eventually breed out the wolfhound stigma."

Naomi shuddered at what could have happened. Who knew what fate had awaited her and Emily if she'd remained their captive.

"How did you get away?"

"Kian had taken out a life insurance policy. They wanted the money, but I was the only one who could sign the papers. Of course, I also needed a bank account to deposit the money. Kian's father, Gerard, barely left my side the day I went to cash the cheque. Because they wanted all the money withdrawn from the account at once, the bank manager insisted on taking me to a private room to make the transaction. I knew it was my only chance, so I faked early labour. People tend to freak out when a pregnant woman starts clutching her belly. Once the ambulance came, Gerard couldn't get near me for paramedics. I legged it from the hospital as soon as I could, with the money safely stashed in my bag, and I ended up here in the hills." The trauma summed up in one brief commentary couldn't ever do justice to the suffering and pain she'd gone through.

Rory put his arms around her and she unfurled to yield to his embrace. "You're so brave. I swear I won't ever let those bastards near you or Emily again. I love you, Naomi. I know I'll never be able to change what happened, but I'll do everything I can to make sure you're happy."

"Thanks, Rory. I...I..." She couldn't get the words out to tell him how much he meant to her. She threw the covers back. "I could really use some fresh air."

Perhaps it was the heightened emotion of finally sharing her burden, and Rory's declaration to her, or reliving that claustrophobic hell, but Naomi needed some space.

"Tonight's a night for firsts. Why don't we go for a run?" If she'd offended him by not reciprocating his sentiment he didn't show it.

"You mean...?" Naomi hadn't dared let her wolf run free since arriving in the hills. The last time she'd done that was with Kian at her side.

"Why not? I think we need to blow a few cobwebs away. That's if you think you can keep up?" Rory sprang out of bed with an amazing burst of energy considering his very physically demanding evening. He seemed determined to prove to her that she need never be on her own again.

"I think you'll find it'll be you who's chasing my tail, Mr Blake." Unashamedly naked, she got up and sashayed towards the door.

The deep growl behind her put an extra wiggle in her walk.

Rory followed her out and watched her shift into her sleek black wolf. His perfect mate. As he gave himself over to his beast, he howled out a warning to those who sought to harm her. If he ever got hold of the O'Connells, he'd rip them limb from limb. Be it in his wolf or human form.

Naomi sauntered back for her playmate and nuzzled his fur. He was the Alpha, her lover. He should be able to protect her. Short of a punch bag to take out his frustrations, this was the next best thing. With a need to outrun his selfish anger, he raced off into the shadows.

Naomi came after him, pitting her stealthy grace against his sheer power. In his peripheral vision, he could see the wisps of her breath spiralling into the cold air as she forged ahead, determined to catch him. Rory snorted, sending his own white breath curling up into the atmosphere.

He led her over the hills, their claws making short work of carving up the cold, hard terrain. Naomi never lost ground. Even when he made a turn towards the woods on the boundary, she kept pace.

The chase awakened something deep inside him — that animal freedom with no responsibilities except the survival of himself and his pack. The spiky silhouettes of barren trees lined his path, like broad strokes of a black marker pen scratched against the silver sky.

He dodged in and out, never slowing, with Naomi always in pursuit. Occasionally, a pair of woodland eyes blinked at him from the darkness — a rabbit, a fox, observing their bizarre courtship.

Rory had no doubt the exhilaration of their illicit run would end in wild sex between him and Naomi. It was like a very enthusiastic bout of foreplay without actual touching.

They crunched through the leaf-littered forest floor until he tired of being the hunted. He looped back the way they came and stopped in a clearing. In all aspects of life he preferred to be the one doing the chasing, but at this moment in time he wanted nothing more than to be caught.

He shifted back into his naked, horny self. Naomi came to a skidding halt seconds later, scooting a bundle of leaves over his bare feet. "You can run, wolf lady, I'll give you that. Now can we go back to bed?"

She shifted back to stand beautifully naked before him. "Not until you say it."

"Say what?" He was hard as hell and ready for round two.

"That I'm as good as you." She gave him a flirty smile. One which said she was looking forward to the future rather than staring back at the past. The run had obviously done wonders for her too.

"That was probably a fluke. I don't think you could keep up with me on a normal day. You know, one where you haven't seduced me on top of a car boot and made me carry you home first." The play fighting wasn't limited to their animal personas. Not when it proved such a turn on. Human or wolf, the scent of Naomi's arousal would always draw him to her.

"I didn't hear you complaining at the time. But, if you're tired, just say and we'll call it a night." She shrugged her shoulders, making her boobs jiggle enough to bring his erection to full strength once more.

He stepped forward and brushed her wild hair from her face. "I'll never be too tired for you, Naomi. I'll race you back. This time the winner stays on top."

She grinned, eyes twinkling as bright as the stars. "You're on."

This was one race he intended to lose.

Chapter Thirteen

The sun shone through the rain on the day of Mia and Caleb's wedding. As chief bridesmaid, Naomi had stayed with Mia at her parents' house the night before. The first night she'd spent away from Rory in weeks. Although the separation seemed odd, it did give her some quality time with the girls. An unusual Halloween night, as they'd spent it doing girly things, like painting their nails and making themselves beautiful for the big day.

As she watched Mia's mother and the hairstylist primp and preen over the bride, Naomi was forced to look away. Once upon a time, she'd been the glowing bride-to-be looking forward to a life with her new husband. With her hair and makeup completed, and Emily happily showing off her dress to everyone who stopped by, Naomi took a much needed time out.

She wandered into one of the many bedrooms. Rory's old room, she guessed, judging by the old football boots lying around, and the faded Nirvana poster on the wall. She smiled, imagining him as a teenager—handsome, no doubt, with that oh-so-serious expression that only she knew how to get rid of.

"You look beautiful." Rory startled her.

"What are you doing here? Shouldn't you be making sure the groom is suited and booted ready for show time?" Naomi moved to the window to watch the caterers buzzing in and out of the large marquee in the grounds.

"Caleb's been ready for hours, and so have I. I couldn't sleep last night for thinking about you." He closed the door and advanced on her, looking hot in his dark grey suit and silver waistcoat.

"What about me?" If his thoughts had been anything like hers last night they were definitely X-rated.

"I was thinking about how you should've been in my bed, naked." Rory ran a hand over her bare shoulder, his touch immediately turning her nipples to pebbles under the silk of her dress.

"You'll just have to wait until tonight." Now he'd started that familiar ache between her legs she found increasingly hard to ignore.

"I really can't. Not unless it's socially acceptable to walk down the aisle with a hard-on." He took her hand and rubbed it against the crotch of his trousers.

The bulge made Naomi's mouth and pussy water. "The wedding is in an hour and I've just had my hair done." She patted her sophisticated up-do.

"I promise not to touch your hair." Rory kissed the skin at the back of her neck. He wasn't playing fair.

"It took ages to get this dress on." The corset-like ties on the bodice had been a bugger to lace through and she didn't have time to redo them.

"I promise not to take your dress off." She could hear the wicked smile in his voice as he reached under her dress and hooked his fingers into her knickers.

He whipped them down her legs, exposing her wet folds to the cool air which made her even more sensitive.

"This is your sister's wedding day." Her head made the protest, but she was already waiting for him.

"Yeah, and the best man's supposed to get it on with the bridesmaid." The rasp of his zipper gave her a slight warning before he slipped in from behind. She leaned over onto the windowsill and let him push deep inside her, almost purring with contentment to be joined with him once more.

"Just because I'm on the pill now doesn't mean you can shag me wherever and whenever you feel like it." Her faux protest didn't fool either of them. After all, Naomi had been the one who made the decision to go on the pill after that night in the car park, when it had seemed lust could easily get the better of her.

"I thought that's exactly what it meant," Rory groaned in her ear as he lifted her skirts up over her bare backside.

Naomi snapped the window blinds shut so the staff outside didn't get an eyeful. Christ, they made each other reckless. This insta-lust connection meant one click of his fingers and she dropped her panties any time, any place, anywhere.

She moaned—her arousal stretching her with ease to accept the deep fill of his cock.

"Fuck, I love you, Naomi." The curious mix of animal passion and romantic sentiment, undid her. She rocked back on his fleshy staff to forge their bodies together from root to tip.

With his hands anchored on her hips, he pulled out and plunged into her again. Each penetration into her channel pushed her further towards bliss. Hard and fast, soft and slow, she took him every way she could.

Their rhythm soon matched their frantic climb for ultimate release.

She bit down on her bottom lip, silencing her special, Rory-induced happy squeals. He moved his hands to brace himself on the window frame. A firm thrust of his hips slammed him into her again, slapping her buttocks against his thighs. She thought he might fuck her right into the wall, until the Blakes had a nice new erotic fresco to decorate the room.

As her body tuned into that frequency that only extremely lucky women had access to, she increased her grip on the sill. If he took her any higher, her French manicure would be ruined for sure. Another clit-clenching thrust. Fuck it. No one would be looking at her nails anyway.

She went with it, riding the wave of ecstasy until it crashed over her, leaving her soaked and breathless. Rory's victorious roar followed in quick succession as he spilled inside her.

"I guess that's one thing you can cross off your list of best man duties," she said with a grin.

He'd certainly stopped her from descending into a well of self-pity, even if she would have to go and clean up again before the ceremony began.

"It's not my fault I find you irresistible. Are you sure you're not some sort of siren-wolf shifter mix?" Rory pressed a kiss into the skin below her earlobe before he withdrew.

Naomi bent to retrieve her panties strewn hussy-like onto the floor, while he zipped his trousers.

"I'm sure. Now shoo and stop distracting me from the big day. It's not all about you, you know." She patted a few loose tendrils of her hair back into place and attempted to regain her dignity. It was difficult to do with her knickers in her hand.

"Now you've had your wicked way with me you're throwing me out?" Rory chortled and spun her around for one last kiss.

Naomi sighed into his comforting embrace, over all too quickly.

"I guess the next time I see you, Ms Duffy, will be down the aisle." He left her with a wink and gave her one last look at his gorgeous backside as he walked out the door.

The joke hit her somewhere deep. Somewhere sensitive that didn't see the funny side. She would never marry again, and no one, not even Rory could change her mind.

* * * *

Rory stood at Caleb's side, butterflies fluttering in his own stomach as they waited for the bridal party on the lawn. A ripple of appreciation carried through the gathered guests when they arrived, but both groom and best man resisted turning around as the wedding march rang out.

Emily appeared first in Rory's peripheral vision, taking her role very seriously as she scattered rose petals to line the bride's path. The 'aww' factor was quickly eclipsed by the 'wow' factor when Naomi arrived.

Even though he'd already seen her, had her in his arms, her beauty still took his breath away. She slipped him a sly smile as she moved to the left hand side of the decorative white arch.

Mia walked up the middle of the gathering on their father's arm, beaming with happiness.

"Christ. I hit the jackpot with your sister, mate," Caleb peacocked beside Rory.

"I know you did and you'd better make sure you never forget what a lucky fecker you are to have her." Rory slapped him on the back, as a congratulations and a warning.

The groom paid little notice as he'd already moved to claim his new wife.

As the registrar welcomed the congregation to celebrate Mia and Caleb's day with them, Rory glanced back at their family and friends. They were blessed. It wasn't the whole big church wedding his parents wanted, studded with the cream of society, but a small group of Mia and Caleb's loved ones. It made it a much more relaxed, informal affair.

His father proudly proclaimed his, 'I do', when asked who was giving Mia away. Rory watched him take a seat beside his mother who had a wriggly Sophie to contend with as well as her running mascara. He hoped her tears were of happiness, not despair, since she and Caleb had long since called a truce. If anything, these days their teasing bordered on flirting. Now here they were being all civilised.

Rory tuned back into the ceremony in time to hear the happy couple exchanging vows. Each 'I do', was followed by matching grins. He might've been jealous if he wasn't swapping the same sickly sweet smiles with the bridesmaid.

Rory imagined standing here in Caleb's shoes, with Naomi playing the part of the blushing bride. *It's not such a stretch, is it?* They loved each other, spent every waking moment they could together, with Emily at the centre of their world. The beginnings of a happy little family.

Whoops and cheers interrupted his fluffy daydream as they were pronounced man and wife, and he was subjected to a full on snog between his sister and his best mate.

At that moment, the heavens opened to dampen their ardour. The guests all scrambled into the marquee for sanctuary from the rain. Mia hitched up her dress and made a run for it with her new husband, and Rory took Naomi's arm to rush her and Emily inside.

"We just about made it," Naomi laughed and shook the raindrops from her hair inside the tent.

"Thank God we got through the ceremony first at least." Rory escorted her to the top table as the others dried themselves off and took their seats. Mia and Caleb were already sitting down along with his parents and the girls.

"Champagne, sir?" A waiter hovered at his side with a tray of champagne flutes.

"Yes, please." He took a glass and necked it back. He needed all the courage he could get for the plans he had in mind for later.

* * * *

Rory barely touched any of the three courses set down in front of him.

Naomi patted his hand. "Don't worry, love. I'm sure you'll be grand."

He stared blankly at her until it dawned on him she thought he was panicking about giving his best man's speech. *Now I am!*

"Ladies and gentlemen. May I have your attention for the speeches," the MC announced him.

Rory gave a nervous cough and got to his feet. "Thank you everyone for coming today as we welcome Caleb into our family. I'd be failing to honour my role here if I didn't dish some dirt on him. But most of you have seen him bare arsed in the pub, so it's no secret he's partial to a bit of manscaping."

The first peals of laughter got him off to a good start and set the tone for the rest of the speeches—a joke here and there, and sentimental in places. They were all worn out by the time the first dance came around.

Caleb and Mia took to the floor to the strains of Shakira's *She-wolf*, busting out moves that left them all gasping.

"I didn't know your sister was double jointed." Naomi cocked her head to one side, watching the hip-defying action.

"Me neither. Caleb's got some moves too apparently." It shouldn't have come as a surprise to Rory that his best mate would shun the traditional first waltz to drop to the floor and do the caterpillar instead.

"What about you?" Naomi asked, mischief written all over her face.

"Oh, I can strut my stuff when the mood calls for it." Rory slid his arm around her waist and pulled her close enough that her hair tickled his nose and her scent called to his beast.

"Can we have the rest of the bridal party up for the next dance please?" the DJ called them to arms, and Rory stopped by the decks for a quick word before he took to the dance floor.

Thankfully, the more respectable slow dance meant all Rory had to do was take Naomi in his arms, and he was an expert in that field. As they twirled around the loved-up newlyweds with Naomi's head resting gently against his chest, Rory couldn't think of a better time and place to do what he had to do.

When the music ended, Rory dropped to one knee in front of his dance partner.

"What are you doing?" Naomi's mouth flopped open in horror.

As the blood pounded in Rory's ears he was vaguely aware of the silence which had descended on the room. Mia stood next to him clinging on to the lapels of Caleb's jacket with tears in her eyes. He much preferred his sister's reaction—especially since he'd stolen some of the limelight on her day.

"Naomi, I love you more than any man could ever love another woman. I can't imagine my life without you or Emily in it. I don't have a ring, but I'm baring my soul to you in front of all these people. Will you marry me?" He took her hand between his trembling fingers and waited for her response.

"No!" she cried out in utter dismay before fleeing the marquee. Leaving Rory humiliated and broken hearted on the dance floor.

Chapter Fourteen

Why would he do this to me? Naomi ran from the reception, away from Rory's very public proposal, out onto the lawn. At least the rain had stopped now. She eyed up the line of trees in the distance and thought hard about shifting into her wolf to escape.

"Mummy?" Emily placed her hand in Naomi's, having followed her out of the tent.

"Hi, sweetheart." She blinked away her tears and forced a smile for her daughter.

"Why are you crying?" Emily screwed up her face, studying her mother closely.

"I'm just very happy for Mia and Caleb." With her little girl clinging to her, Naomi started walking in case Rory was next to come looking for her.

She couldn't face him. Marriage wasn't something she'd contemplated since Kian. Something she would never contemplate. Rory should have known her well enough to understand that.

There'd been no clue he'd planned to propose and with the absence of a ring she'd have to conclude it was a spur of the moment decision. Perhaps he'd got carried away by the romance of the occasion.

"Are you cross with Rory, Mummy?" A small voice chimed up to remind Naomi she wasn't alone.

"Yes. No. He did something silly. I'm sure we'll make up later." In truth she didn't know how they could come back from this if they wanted such different things.

Naively she'd thought they were happy simply being in each other's company. If Rory wanted a wife, children of his own, he was going down an altogether different path to hers.

The thought unsettled her as they turned around the corner of the house. What if her finally settled life here in Olcan Hills with Emily was about to be thrown into turmoil again? She wasn't sure she could survive the loss of another partner. And Rory was a huge part of their lives here. They needed to do some serious talking away from all this wedded bliss.

A sudden yank around her waist winded her. A large hand clamped over her mouth and muffled her scream as she was lifted off her feet. She struggled and kicked against the restraint but could only watch in horror as the same fate befell her daughter, and she was carried away like a bundle of rags. The two men were scruffy, their faces partially hidden by the hoods of their sweatshirts. Naomi's captor smelt of cigarettes and body odour.

It triggered an unwelcome feeling of familiarity. Gerard O'Connell. He'd finally come for her.

Her mind raced through the possibilities as she was dragged towards a beat up van parked at the end of the drive with the engine running. She could shift, take him on in her wolf guise, but that wouldn't help her get Emily back. Besides, she still bore the scars from the last time she'd tried to take them on as a pack.

The look of fear in her daughter's eyes would haunt her forever and was enough for Naomi to swear her revenge on these bastards. She wouldn't let them get away with whatever fucked-up plans they had for her.

O'Connell tossed her into the back of the van. She hit the rusted floor with a thud, banging her head in the process. Emily was huddled in the corner, her arms hugging her knees.

Naomi ignored the throbbing at her temple to console her daughter, pulling her onto her lap. "It's all right, sweetheart. I'll get us out of here."

If she had to fight to the death to wrench her child from their clutches, she would. They underestimated how far a pissed off mama wolf would go to protect her cub. They were about to find out. The morons hadn't bothered to tie them up, or gag them, and Naomi knew this could be her last chance to summon help before they took her over the border.

"Emily, I need you to be very brave now. We have to make as much noise as possible so Rory and the others will hear and come get us. Okay?"

Emily nodded but didn't make a move to leave her. The speeding van hit a pothole in the road sending them sprawling onto the dirty floor once more. Time was running out. She took Emily's hand and helped her to her feet.

"Help!" Naomi pounded on the side panels of their prison.

Emily copied her with tiny fists and screamed along with her. They punched, they yelled, they kicked. Naomi even tried the handle of the door just in case, but they were trapped, destined for Christ-knew-what.

She carried on protesting until her throat ached and the palms of her hands were red and raw. The sudden screech of brakes sent both of them hurtling into the solid panel separating them from the driver. Emily started to cry.

Naomi checked her over for cuts and bruises but saw nothing serious. The tears were probably a reaction to the whole traumatic experience. She couldn't blame her. If her body wasn't thriving on adrenaline right now she'd probably give into tears too.

While trying to soothe Emily, Naomi stayed on alert for whatever else was about to be inflicted on them. Outside, she heard raised voices. She wondered if it was more wolfhound scum come to gloat, or even separate them. She cuddled Emily tighter.

A crash on the roof thundered from above, followed by the heavy padding of what sounded like claws scratching the top of the van. With her baby in her arms, Naomi scrabbled as far back into the corner as she could, never taking her eyes off the door. Waiting for whatever was about to burst in.

Emily buried her head in her mother's bosom, her sniffs and sobs the only things preventing Naomi from hyperventilating as she fought to keep them both calm.

The driver's door opened and slammed shut. Gravel crunched underfoot as someone rounded the side of the van and stopped at the rear. Naomi held her breath.

The squeak as the doors opened echoed around the van and the sudden glare of the sun temporarily blinded her. She held a hand up to shield her eyes from the light and squinted into the brightness.

"Caleb?" Her best friend's other half stood naked at her escape route.

"Come on. Quick!" he beckoned, not making any effort to cover his modesty. Putting two and two together, she figured out it was him she'd heard stalking on the roof.

She didn't need to be told twice. She scooped Emily up and bolted out. Mia was there too, waiting to give her a hug. "Are you okay?"

"I'm fine. What happened?" Naomi hoisted Emily onto her hip, ignoring the aches and pains crying out all over her battered body.

"Rory came out after you in time to see those bastards bundling you into the van. He called Caleb just before he threw himself in the middle of the road." Mia nodded towards the front of the van.

"What?" Naomi needed to see what was happening, to make sure he was all right.

"Can you take Emily up to the house for me?" At least knowing her daughter was safe would ease her mind a fraction. Naomi handed Emily over, assuring her Mia would look after her, and made her way to the melee still going on in the road.

"You can keep this bitch, but the girl is ours." Obviously O'Connell was oblivious to the fact his cargo had already been unloaded as he sneered at Rory.

Rory stood firm, blocking his path. "No one fucks with my family," he growled, his brown eyes shining with the amber glow of his wolf.

The hairs on the back of Naomi's neck stood to attention. She preferred to think it was a primitive reaction to his wolf, and not a simpering response to being referred to as 'his family'.

"This is my family by blood and no one can stop me from taking the child." Gerard summoned his accomplices from the van. The passenger door opened and Naomi recognised Kian's elder brothers as they flanked their father.

Caleb, now wearing trousers at least, came to stand with Rory.

"This is your last chance to walk away unscathed. You've threatened my girlfriend, attempted to kidnap her and her daughter and I already have a string of charges on file against you, Mr O'Connell. It would be in your best interests to leave. Now." The threat was there in the vibrato of Rory's growl.

"You're a peeler? Well, what are you gonna do? Arrest me?" The O'Connell trio sniggered together.

"I'm also the Alpha of the Olcan Hills pack. We have our own methods of justice." Rory dropped his claws in a show of dominance.

Naomi swallowed hard. She knew the O'Connells wouldn't back down from a scrap.

"Fine by me." The leader of the opposition pulled off his jacket and started to loosen his clothing.

One by one, the O'Connells changed into their mangy alter egos.

"Let's party." Caleb didn't take much persuading to strip again and switch back to his wolf.

"Rory. Be careful," she pleaded as he began his transition.

He fixed her with those cold yellow eyes. "This needs to end, now."

Rory embraced his beast, along with all the anger and frustration he needed to release. He'd made an epic mistake, and nearly lost Naomi and Emily for good. When he'd seen his girls chucked into the van like trash, he'd wanted to tear the O'Connells limb from limb. He still did. Only his humanity prevented him.

In his wolf form he had no such qualms. They were on his territory, threatening his pack, and worst of all, they weren't even wolves. They were wannabes who needed to respect his authority.

Rory took a step forward and growled his warning this time. The mutts showed no signs of submission. Caleb's grey wolf, Rory's Beta in many respects despite his reluctance to officially accept the position, stayed beside him.

The O'Connells barked and snarled, saliva forming at the corners of their mouths. They padded a circle around Rory and Caleb. The younger hounds snapped at their heels like annoying puppies. Rory ignored the sharp teeth biting his hind legs and kept his focus on the elder. A motley specimen, his grey fur was marked with scars and bald patches, and Rory suspected him to be a wily foe. After all, he had bide his time, waiting for the perfect opportunity to snatch Naomi.

Naomi. He glanced back to make sure she was still there. The blood and dirt smeared across her beautiful face temporarily distracted him from the fight.

O'Connell launched at him, sinking his rotten teeth into the scruff of Rory's neck. He yelped and vigorously shook his head until the fleabag loosened his grip. *Game on.*

Caleb danced toe to toe with the others, drawing them away to leave the pack masters to it. Rory leant back on his haunches and propelled himself into full attack. He side swiped the wolfhound and felled him like a mighty oak in an angry storm. They hit the dirt at the side of the road and rolled, fur flying as they clashed.

Fangs and claws sliced through flesh during the skirmish, battling for dominance. O'Connell took the upper hand as they landed, with Rory pinned under his sheer weight. Dog drool dripped onto Rory as O'Connell curled his lip and bared his teeth. He wasn't used to being on the receiving end of an act of aggression and he sure as hell wasn't about to play the submissive. Rory lifted his head and chomped down on the dog's ear.

The element of surprise and acute pain left O'Connell yelping, and gave Rory enough room to throw him off to get back to his feet. As the wolfhound retreated to lick his wounds, Rory checked on Caleb who was tossing the other huge canines into the dirt like he was swatting flies.

"Rory!" He heard Naomi's scream in time to see O'Connell running full pelt in her direction.

She dropped into her black wolf to take the force of the attack. Even though he was running hard enough for his lungs to burst, Rory couldn't get there in time. The hound ploughed into her and catapulted her to the other side of the road. Lying winded, Naomi was helpless as O'Connell lunged for her throat.

Rory charged, fuelled by his wrath. The woman he loved was being mauled, lying bleeding on the ground after a lifetime of emotional torture at the hands of this man. Whether she wanted to be with Rory or not, she deserved to live the rest of her life in peace. Free from the shadow of the O'Connells.

Rory rammed his head into the hound's ribs, knocking him away from his prey. He dodged O'Connell's muzzle snapping at him only to feel the searing pain of his claws in his hind quarters. The penalty he paid for not being able to protect his mate.

Rory lunged back and snapped his jaws shut around a mouthful of the hound's throat.

Images of a bloodied Naomi and a tearful Emily swam in his head. They couldn't go through this ever again. It ended now. With a vicious growl, Rory shook his head, his fangs ripping the flesh from O'Connell's throat.

Caleb's scrap with the others fell silent as O'Connell crumpled to the ground, blood pumping from his fatal wound to soak into the hills. The youngsters whimpered and nudged their father's body. As his life ebbed away, O'Connell morphed back into his human form. His sons changed back too, to cradle him in his last moments.

Once they saw the threat had passed, Caleb and Rory assumed their more sociably acceptable appearance to check on Naomi. Rory used what was left of her dress to cover her naked and bruised body. The bite on her neck wasn't too deep, but he'd make sure she got a tetanus jab at least.

"What happened?" she mumbled as she came to.

"Rory took him out. Gerard O'Connell won't bother you ever again." Caleb patted him on the back, but Rory wasn't proud of what he'd done. He'd simply removed the threat blighting Naomi's life.

"You didn't have to fucking kill him!" the younger of the two brothers yelled at him, tears streaking his face.

"I warned you. Now pack up your shit and get out of here." In a callous act, Rory kicked the deceased's foot.

Deep down he sympathised with their loss, but he couldn't show any weakness now.

"We could have you done for murder."

"Yeah? Try it. To all intents and purposes this was an animal attack. I'm sure my colleagues would be much more interested in your activities than mine." He hoped the plans for Emily was more their father's obsession than theirs. Hopefully scrotes like them would stick to their money making schemes rather than care about their lineage.

Between them they manoeuvred O'Connell's body into the van. If hounds were anything like the wolf community, they'd rather deal with their dead than leave it to strangers.

"You'll get yours." Junior couldn't resist one last goad before they retreated.

"Try it," Caleb growled.

Around them, a chorus of similar wolf warnings sounded. Rory watched as the shifter wedding guests assembled and circled the O'Connell boys in their wolf forms. Pride swelled in his chest at the support and bravery of his pack. He hoped Naomi's tormenters finally realised they were up against more than a single mother and her daughter now.

The surviving O'Connells got into the van and slammed the doors shut. The pack moved aside to let them pass, uniting in a bone chilling howl to see them off.

Chapter Fifteen

"Do you think they'll come back?" Naomi had to ask the question as Rory pressed the sponge to her skin.

Naked, physically and emotionally drained, they'd returned to the Blakes' house to tend to their wounds. Naomi winced as the warm bath water soaked her cuts and grazes, but she found some comfort as she sat between Rory's strong thighs in the bath tub.

"No," he said firmly enough for her to believe him.

The lengths he'd gone to to protect her and Emily was mind-blowing. "I'm sorry you had to do that."

"None of this was your fault, Naomi. I'd do it again if I had to. There's only one part of today I'd change if I could. I didn't realise you felt so strongly about not marrying me." He squeezed another trickle of water over her shoulders.

"You know it's not you. I love you, Rory. I just...I just can't imagine ever marrying again. Can we forget it happened and carry on the way we were?" All she'd ever wanted was to live a normal life. Well, as normal as a wolf shifter and her cub could be.

"If that's what you want." She couldn't see his face to work out if he was scowling, but she suspected saying she loved him still wasn't enough for him.

She sighed and leant back so he could lather her hair with shampoo. As he massaged her scalp, she almost drifted off to sleep. On any other night it could've counted as foreplay. The day had certainly taken its toll, and she would much prefer climbing into bed after their bath rather than joining the party downstairs.

Rory's parents had opened up their house for all the guests to recover from the excitement and get cleaned up. The reception was to carry on downstairs in an attempt to save Mia and Caleb's day. Mia and her mother had taken Emily and Sophie far from the goings on with the O'Connells, and were no doubt spoiling them somewhere in the house with leftover desserts.

Once Naomi had patched herself up enough to make sure she didn't terrify her daughter, she'd check on Emily again, despite Rory's assurances she was fine.

She slid farther down Rory's long legs to let the lavender scented suds cover her chest and neck, while he rinsed out her hair. He had all the qualities a woman could ever want in her man—a fierce protector who could be tender and loving when called for.

She only wished they could find a way to continue together without compromising their beliefs and make their future brighter.

* * * *

Once they were cleaned up and soothed their aches as best they could, Naomi and Rory dressed for the party. Rory still had some of his old clothes in his closet to choose from, and Naomi borrowed one of Mia's pre-Sophie designer dresses.

An anxious crowd gathered at the foot of the staircase as they made their way down, hand in hand.

"Are you okay?" Mia rushed up to meet them before they hit the bottom step.

"We're fine," Rory assured her, although Naomi had witnessed the bruising around his ribs to know he had to be in some pain.

Mia fussed, tracing her fingers over the marks O'Connell had left on her throat.

"It could've been much worse." Naomi brushed her away.

The few minor injuries they sported were nothing compared to a man having lost his life. An act, although made in self-defence, was one she was sure Rory wouldn't have taken lightly. It left her in no doubt about the strength of his feelings for her.

"I'm so sorry I wasn't there for you, sis. I didn't know anything was going on until it was too late." Liam was next in the queue to check on her.

"It's not your fault. They took us all by surprise. I'm just glad Rory was there to save me." She squeezed Rory's hand and offered him a teary smile.

"And Caleb too," she added as the Beta bounded up to his Alpha.

"Thanks for the back-up, mate." Rory dropped her hand to squash Caleb in a bear hug and lift him clean off his feet.

"Oww! Take it easy. I think I've added a few new battle scars today." Caleb was half-laughing, half-wincing, and clearly experiencing the same after effects of the fight as they were.

"You and me both." Rory released him and proceeded to double over.

"Poor baby." Naomi patted his shoulder in sympathy.

"Mummy!" An Emily missile launched at Naomi, winding her in an over enthusiastic hug.

"Hey, sweetie." She settled for a kiss, unsure if she was physically capable of lifting her daughter.

Emily frowned. "Have the bad men gone?"

It broke Naomi's heart that this was the child's own family she was talking about. Her own grandfather had been slaughtered to keep her safe. A shiver rippled over her skin.

"They're all gone. Rory chased them away." She plastered on a happy smile, determined to convince her there was no reason to worry.

It worked. Emily turned her attention to Rory, throwing her arms around his waist. He winced but endured the embrace. They were adorable together and it was obvious how much they cared for one another.

The strains of music started farther down the hall and the crowd began to dissipate.

"I can't apologise enough for ruining your wedding." After all their planning, Mia and Caleb's day had been spoilt because of her.

"You did not ruin it. We're married aren't we? And you and Emily are both safe, that's all that matters." Mia welled up as she spoke and almost set Naomi off too after such an emotionally fraught day.

"We were never going to have a traditional wedding anyway, were we?" Caleb's grin eased Naomi's burden of guilt.

"I think we could do with a drink." Rory's thoughts met with everyone's approval.

"Good idea."

"I think we deserve one."

"Where's the bar."

Naomi was merely grateful to finally step down and set foot on solid ground.

"Hey, Rory. Are you okay?" Naomi lagged behind the others to have a quiet moment with her man.

"Yeah. It's been a long day, that's all." Ever since they'd returned to the house he'd been quiet, distant even.

He had more than enough reason to be introspective after the events, and she'd done her own share of deep thinking when Rory had tended to her in the bath. The fear flowing in her veins came when she thought he might finally have had enough of her. In the past few hours she'd publicly rejected him and been the reason he'd taken a man's life.

"Talk to me, Rory." His reluctance to open up to her, share his worries made her all the more anxious.

She couldn't begin to contemplate life without him. Not when it was only beginning. He'd saved her. She loved him. What more was there?

"Rory, I don't want anything except you and Emily. I don't understand what the problem is."

"The problem is I need a commitment from you. Some fucking indication that you've stopped running. That someday I won't turn around and find you and Emily have done a disappearing act." The vein standing out at his temple looked like it would pop. She'd had no idea he was so stressed at the thought of losing her.

She cupped his face in her hands. "I have no intention of leaving you. I might not want to marry again, but I do know I'll never love anyone more than I love you."

All along she'd thought he was caught up in the idea of marriage, when he simply wanted to be sure of her devotion to him. There was one way they could have their happy ever after.

Naomi got down on one knee on the cold marble floor as fast as her aching joints would allow. A bemused Rory looked on as she took his hand.

"Rory Blake, would you make me the happiest woman in the Hills and let me move in with you?" With the eyes of their friends and family boring into the back of her head, she actually wasn't certain he'd agree. She'd definitely have to make it up to him later for dashing his hopes when he'd been in the same agonising position.

He sandwiched her hand between both of his and yanked her back onto her feet. "I'd love to."

Rory dipped her back into a Hollywood style kiss. As his lips claimed hers, and his hand moved to the small of her back to support her, Naomi finally knew she was safe.

Epilogue

"Hi. We thought you might like us to take Emily for an ice cream, or a sleepover, or anything that'll give you guys some time on your own." Mia stood on the doorstep with Caleb and Sophie in tow.

Naomi could've kissed them all. "Thank you. Thank you. Thank you. Emily pack your bags, you're spending the night at Sophie's."

Rory popped his head around the living room door. "Really?"

Naomi nodded, barely containing her glee.

"I'll help her pack," he volunteered and made a dash for her bedroom.

Naomi invited their friends in to wait, but it wasn't long before Emily came to join them with her pink princess overnight bag.

"That bad, huh?" Mia sidled up to Naomi.

She rolled her eyes. "This living together hasn't been a picnic so far. There are definitely three people in this relationship.

"Are you getting cock blocked by a four year old, bro?" Caleb joined the whispering in the corner as the children were distracted by Emily's new walkie-talkie set—another attempt to get her to stay in her own bed instead of crawling in between Naomi and Rory every night.

Rory winced. Naomi knew he wouldn't admit it but that's exactly what her daughter was doing. In the first few days after they'd moved in with Rory, Naomi and Emily had taken the master bedroom with Rory on the couch until they'd finished decorating the little girl's room.

He'd done a wonderful job creating the perfect girly retreat with all her favourite toys to make her feel at home. But the separation anxiety had proved more exhausting than they'd anticipated. The only way of pacifying Emily was having her mother beside her.

When they finally thought they'd made the transition and got through one night with everyone in their own beds, the nightmares started. After all she'd been through it was understandable. It just wasn't how Naomi and Rory had imagined their cosy love nest.

The snatched moments they had together were less than when they'd lived at separate addresses. Yet, as frustrated as Rory surely was, he hadn't complained.

"I guess that's parenthood for you," was Rory's response to Caleb.

In every way but one, Rory was Emily's father and he did a wonderful job looking after her. Naomi thanked her lucky stars every day for having him in their lives.

As Emily gathered her belongings without a single qualm about staying away from her mother tonight, Naomi wondered how much of her recent behaviour could be down to attention seeking.

"Have you noticed Emily doesn't seem fazed at all about leaving us tonight?" she made her observation to Rory.

"Hmm. Far from traumatised, she's excited about it." Rather than lingering on it, he laughed. The deep, warm, rumble, awakened Naomi's libido in anticipation of a night free from interruption.

"Looks like she's got everything. We won't keep you." Naomi ushered the band to the front door, and virtually shoved them outside, much to Caleb's amusement.

"I think you're onto a sure thing," he shouted back to Rory.

"I bloody well hope so!" The first signs of his frustration manifested as they waved everyone off.

"We've got all night, you know." Naomi smiled sweetly as they hovered in the doorway, with Rory sliding his hand down her back to grab her arse.

"I intend making up for lost time." Without warning, Naomi was literally swept off her feet into Rory's arms and he kicked the front door shut.

She draped herself like a scarf around his neck and found his lips with hers, kissing him like it was their first time. Rory stalked to the bedroom, carrying her like his prey he was set to devour. Naomi shuddered, excitement chasing away any residual weariness.

When he set her down on the bed, they raced to see who could get naked first. Naomi giggled as buttons pinged off and rained down on the wooden floor, and shirts were balled up and thrown across the room. Rory pounced onto the bed, bouncing her against the mattress, and covering her bare flesh with his.

She sighed at the skin to skin contact that beaded her nipples against his chest. This was all she needed to call home.

"Now, I know you don't like your wrists being held, but how about your fingers?" Rory slipped his fingers in between hers and brought them up to his lips.

"Fingers are fine." She found it hard to object as he took her index finger into his mouth and sucked on it.

"And elbows?" He lifted her arm to kiss the sensitive skin on the inside of her arm.

Naomi laughed. "A little ticklish maybe, but elbows are on the tick list too."

"What about shoulders?" He pressed his lips onto the curve of her shoulder.

"No problems there either."

He stopped asking permission as he moved to caress her collarbone with kisses. Before she knew it he'd covered her nipple too, teasing her with his tongue until she was completely at his mercy. When he withdrew his ministrations, she whimpered like an abandoned puppy.

"Naomi, I don't want you to be scared anymore." Rory's playful nature she'd been so enjoying suddenly turned serious.

"I'm not," she said with absolute certainty. After everything he'd done for her she refused to let fear claim another second of her existence.

"I want you to trust me one hundred per cent."

"I do." *Shut up and get on with it. I'm horny here.*

He reached over to his night stand to rummage in the drawer. "Prove it."

A pair of handcuffs swung from his fingers. "Tell me to stop and I'll stop, but I think you owe it to yourself to try."

Naomi gulped. Could she really expunge the O'Connell spectre for good? "Okay. I'll give it a shot."

Rory fastened one end of the restraints around her wrist, and the other around a bar of the brass headboard.

She took a deep breath and closed her eyes. Bad move. She was back in that hell, chains stripping the skin from her wrists and ankles. Waiting, crying for help that never came.

"Look at me," Rory demanded, pulling her back.

She opened her eyes and forced herself to focus on the love staring back at her.

"I'm not trying to hurt you, or make you uncomfortable. Just think of this as a trust exercise. You have to trust that I know exactly what you want, and need." The cheeky wink he gave her returned them to the fun aspect of the night's activities.

Rory dipped his head until they were nose to nose, his breath hot on her lips, and Naomi's past was eclipsed by the promise of a hot future. She almost forgot she was cuffed to the bed when he closed his mouth on hers and sent his tongue on a mission to save her from her own thoughts.

Only a real masochist would abandon this passion to wallow in the recollection of ill-treatment at the hands of the O'Connells. Rory was right. She needed to trust him, and herself. In the interests of their relationship, and her own sanity, tonight she intended to stop thinking and concentrate on feeling. Starting from now.

He moved to place a tender kiss on the skin below the handcuff, running his tongue across the scars she imagined were still there. It was an acknowledgement of her issues but also a promise to help her to work through them.

Naomi saw no need to fight against her confinement as she surrendered to her captor's control. Every soft caress released a little more of the tension in her limbs until she was no longer a victim of her memories, simply a woman being made love to.

Rory nuzzled into her neck, and took the weight of her breast in his hands. He rolled her nipple between his thumb and finger and pinched. The throbbing pleasure he left in his wake certainly wasn't regionalised as it darted straight down to drench her pussy in desire.

Naomi moaned and shifted on the bed so her mound brushed against his steely erection. Like a rose blossoming in the sun, she opened up to slide along his thick length.

Rory groaned and tensed, a shudder running from his shoulder blades down his back, but he wasn't going to give in easily. He stroked the flat of his hand down her belly, and brushed his palm in between her legs. She bucked against him, yearning for completion.

He filled her aching hole with his fingers, a temporary replacement for the real deal. As he pushed deep inside her, Naomi clawed his back with her free hand. He teased her inner walls, simulating the role of his cock with his digits, stretching her, filling her. She ground her pelvis, moving her hips in small circles to maximise the effect he was having on her clit.

It was only then she cursed her shackles. She wanted him. Any other time she would wrap her body around his and bury his head in her cleavage until he could hold back no longer. This way, she was at a disadvantage and totally on the receiving end of such injustice. Patience never was her virtue.

Rory tortured her further with his nimble fingers, the rapid rhythm of flicking against her nub bending her into a back-breaking arch of sexual pressure. She was nearly there. One more buzz from her Rory sex aid and she'd hit the ceiling.

At the last second, he withdrew. Just when she thought she'd come tumbling back down from her high, he rammed his cock into her slippery entrance to catch her.

This time she could close her eyes without fear. She let the overwhelming sensation of her submission sweep over her. Behind closed lids, there was no darkness or dread stealing her happiness, only the brilliant light and joy of her climax.

Rory forged on through the clench and release of her inner muscles pulsing around his dick. Her juices lubricated his path, letting him slide in and out with ease. He couldn't have wished for more from Naomi tonight. His bold experiment could've gone so badly wrong, but her cries of ecstasy told him he'd got it just right.

There were no signs of resistance, or reluctance, since he'd put the cuffs on and he hoped the spectre of her earlier life had left for good. It certainly felt like it as she coated his erection with her cream. Now they could move on and build on their already fantastic relationship.

He reached up to unlock the cuffs and tested her by pinning her wrists to the bed with his hands. Naomi responded by hitching her knees up to her chest, inviting him deeper.

Rory growled as he plunged inside her, her willingness driving him on. He grasped her ankles and placed them over his shoulder, lifting her butt off the bed so he could further his exploration.

Naomi moaned that gratifying little sound that meant she wasn't done yet. He latched his mouth around her perky pink nipple, sucking and bathing the tip with his tongue. The taste of her freedom was sexy and sweet all at the same time.

He kneaded the cheeks of her arse and opened her up to her limit. Naomi clutched him to her chest and screamed as he slammed her into another orgasm. The current of her climax crashing around his shaft carried him into his own release. He emptied every ounce of love he had for her until he had nothing left to give. For now.

Side by side on the bed, they panted, stunned and drained by their epic demonstration of commitment to one another.

"I think it's fair to say we've laid one more demon to rest," Naomi eventually drew enough breath to say.

"Does that mean—" It was an on-going joke now that every time they made love now, he proposed to her.

"No, I'm not going to marry you." She'd stopped being mad about it a long time ago. In fact she might take it as an insult if he suddenly stopped asking.

"It's not my fault I get carried away in the moment." He reached across to tease her nipple to a point, marvelling at how quickly he could arouse her.

"We both know it's not gonna happen. Although..." She drifted off, leaving him hanging on to the coattails of hope.

"Although what?" He turned onto his side, inwardly screaming for an answer.

Naomi rolled over to face him. "Marriage is out of the question, but that doesn't mean a family is."

A choir of angels sang in his head. Fireworks exploded as all his Christmases came at once. "You're pregnant?"

"No. Not yet." She was quick to cool his jets. "It doesn't mean I can't be in the future. Although after the trauma of my pregnancy with Emily there's no promise it will be an easy ride. If we decide that we want a baby, I'll need your support to get me through. I need some happy memories to replace the dark ones, and, we do seem to have this dual parenting licked."

Rory could've cried with happiness. He would do everything he could do make sure the future mother of his children was comfortable. He'd be so attentive she'd probably get sick of him before the nine months were over. "Well, maybe we should make the most of this quiet time before the house is full of screaming children."

"What did you have in mind? A board game? A nice relaxing bath?" Naomi's gorgeous smile stirred his baby maker back to life.

"I thought maybe we could put in some extra practice." He stroked his fingers along the indent of her hip, picturing her with his baby hoisted there, the image of domestic bliss.

"Hmm. Maybe we should try something new."

His ears perked up.

"I think it's your turn to learn the importance of trust." She swung his cuffs on her finger, sending his imagination into porno overdrive.

"I'm ready and willing. Show me what you got, sweetheart." He lay back and reflected on what a lucky guy he was as Naomi straddled him.

Now he'd have everything he'd ever wanted— Naomi, Emily and a child of his own—a family.

About the Author

Jorja Lovett is a British author with both Irish and Scottish roots, which makes for a very dry sense of humour. Writing since she was old enough to wield a pen, it wasn't until she joined her crit group, UCW, that she pursued her passion seriously.

Now, with Joe Manganiello as her permanent muse, if she can leave the pause button on her Magic Mike dvd long enough, she hopes to spend the rest of her days writing steamy romances.

Jorja Lovett loves to hear from readers. You can find her contact information, website details and author profile page at http://www.totallybound.com.

Totally Bound Publishing

Home of Erotic Romance